'So the hospital is a family affair?'

Craig put his hands on Emma's shoulders. Startled, she glanced up, her hazel-green eyes apprehensive.

'I really do understand your feelings about the future of the hospital, but that doesn't mean I go along with them. You can't make the clock stand still, you know, especially in medicine. As it stands, the cottage hospital is not much more than a glorified convalescent home.'

Emma's face was scarlet and her eyes blazed. 'How dare you call it that?'

Clare Lavenham was a Londoner, but has lived mostly in Suffolk. She is widowed with two grown-up children. She has written articles, short stories and one-act plays, but her work as a hospital librarian led to her writing LOVE ON CALL medical romances. She gets her backgrounds from her library work, and consults various medical friends when necessary. Her favourite occupations, apart from writing, are walking in the country and gardening.

Recent titles by the same author:

HEARTS AT SEA
LOVE IN A MIST
SISTER AT HILLSIDE

HOSPITAL
AT RISK

BY
CLARE LAVENHAM

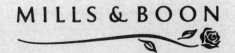

MILLS & BOON

MILLS & BOON, the Rose Device and
LOVE ON CALL are trademarks of the publisher.
Harlequin Mills & Boon Limited,
Eton House, 18-24 Paradise Road, Richmond, Surrey TW9 1SR
This edition published by arrangement with Harlequin Enterprises B.V.

© Clare Lavenham 1995

ISBN 0 263 79260 9

*Set in Times 11 on 12 pt. by
Rowland Phototypesetting Limited
Bury St Edmunds, Suffolk*

03-9508-43444

Made and printed in Great Britain

CHAPTER ONE

IT WAS a warm, sunny day, stolen from summer and inserted into the calendar at the end of October, perhaps to cheer people up before November arrived with its cold grey mists. As Emma crunched along the beach she noticed that there was even someone swimming. A dark head of unknown sex appeared now and then, cleaving strongly through the water and barked at furiously by a large dog leaping about at the edge of the waves.

Emma noted it briefly, marvelled that anyone could be so tough and promptly forgot it.

She always enjoyed her early morning walk along the beach after coming off duty. Even when there was no real wind—rare on the East Anglian coast—there was usually enough breeze to blow away the traumas of the night and give her an appetite for breakfast.

This morning a brisk north-easterly was driving tiny white clouds across the sky and sending her chestnut-brown hair whirling about her head. It was just long enough to be folded into a pleat for work but she always loosened it as soon as she got home. Tramping along in jeans and a big greeny-blue sweater, she bore no resemblance to a neat and efficient staff nurse, which was the image she presented at Saxham cottage hospital.

She had been walking for about ten minutes

when her attention was caught by something going on at the foot of the sandy cliffs about fifty yards ahead. It was a Saturday morning and two boys, who would otherwise have been at school, were busy there, working with buckets, spades and bare hands in the loose sand.

Emma quickened her steps. If they were doing what she suspected, it was not only forbidden by the coastal authorities but extremely perilous.

There were big notices at intervals—THESE CLIFFS ARE DANGEROUS. KEEP AWAY—but within a few seconds she was near enough to have her fears confirmed.

'What on earth are you up to?' she demanded.

The boys looked at her in surprise, their expressions innocent. They were both about ten, old enough to know better.

'Making a cave,' said the fair one.

'So we can have a picnic in it,' the dark boy said helpfully.

'Shall I tell you what you're really doing? Deliberately undermining the cliff, and on this coast that's a major crime.'

'It's only going to be a little cave—just big enough for us to crawl into, isn't it, Pete?'

The fair one backed him up vigorously. 'Kevin's right—it'll be just big enough for us to——'

'Get buried in,' Emma finished for him.

They looked at her mutinously and she wished she didn't have to spoil their fun. They quite obviously thought she was making a fuss about nothing and she had a nasty feeling that as soon as she was out of sight they would resume digging.

'I'm serious,' she told them gravely. 'I'm sure you've been warned at school and at home about these cliffs being unsafe. It's the easiest thing in the world to start a fall of sand, so please do be sensible and find something else to do.'

They exchanged glances and then turned two blank faces towards her. Pete said, 'OK,' and Kevin nodded. Moving at a snail's pace they began to collect the tools. Emma rewarded them with a smile of commendation and continued her walk along the beach.

But she still felt uneasy.

It had been her plan to go as far as some wooden steps which the local council had erected to enable people to reach the top of the cliffs without being tempted by a more adventurous route. She had intended to climb up these and return to her home by the cliff path.

A few yards past the spot where the excavators had been working a considerable cliff-fall hid the view ahead. The big mass of sand, earth and stones had been there for some time, a grim reminder of how unstable these cliffs were. Before rounding it, Emma glanced back, and saw the boys apparently continuing to get ready to depart. She ought to have found the sight satisfactory, but somehow she didn't.

The steps came into view, but at the base of them she came to a halt. It was no good kidding herself that she could go calmly home without checking what those two young devils were up to. With a sigh, she began to retrace her steps.

As soon as she had rounded the cliff-fall she knew she had made the right decision. Kevin and

Pete were digging harder than ever, as though to make up for lost time, and one of them had his head right inside the tiny cave they had hollowed out,

It would take only a small fall of sand to give them a fright and perhaps worse.

Emma began to run. She had nearly reached them when it happened. A little higher up the cliff, a mixture of earth and sand which had been loosely held together by coarse grass shifted suddenly. Slowly at first, it began to slide down to beach level, preceded by a cataract of small stones.

Pete, who was still outside the cave, shouted a warning, but his friend was trapped. The only parts of him still visible were two thin legs in tattered jeans.

Gasping, Emma reached the scene. Wasting no time in recriminations, she seized a spade and began frantically digging, helped by Pete who, although at first frozen with horror, had somehow managed to pull himself together.

At first it seemed a hopeless task. As soon as they shifted a few bucketfuls, more sand came down, and it didn't help that the imprisoned child was frenziedly kicking.

When he stopped kicking, Emma's heart nearly stopped too. If only someone big and strong would arrive and help them, the ultimate disaster might even now be avoided.

What actually arrived was the big black and white dog she had seen earlier. It flung itself enthusiastically into the task of digging, sending sand flying everywhere—into their eyes and noses and mouths. It was a help, but not nearly as much as was needed.

Emma and Pete were both too absorbed to notice heavy footsteps pounding along the shingle. The first she knew of the dog's owner having joined them was when two strong hands took the spade from her and began shovelling at twice her own speed. Vaguely she was aware that the man was almost naked, and a small part of her mind— working independently—recalled the swimmer she had seen.

She did what she could to help and gradually more of Kevin became visible. Suddenly the man abandoned digging.

'Help me draw him out,' he ordered her. 'Take it slowly or we'll do more harm than good.' He took a firm grip on one of the stick-like legs. Very carefully, pausing now and then to clear away sand, they pulled the child free. To Emma, holding her breath with anxiety, it seemed to take ages, though it was no more than a few seconds. Pete burst into loud, childish sobs as he saw the still, blue-tinged face of his friend.

'Can you do resuscitation?' the man asked urgently.

'Yes.'

'Then we'll take it in turns. I'll start on the chest and you can follow with mouth-to-mouth.'

As he began with a thump on the chest, she hurried to wipe away the sand from Kevin's face. When her turn came she felt herself being watched critically, and didn't blame him for not being quite certain of her competence. They worked rhythmically, not speaking, and suddenly their reward came. The boy began to breathe.

Emma sat back on her heels and, for the first time, really looked at the stranger with whom she had just saved a life. She saw a lean face, still showing the remains of summer's tan, a straight nose and square chin. His dark hair was plastered wetly to his head and his eyes were as grey as the sea in winter, but there was nothing cold about them. They were warm and smiling and full of triumph.

'We did well,' he said, and gave her arm a little pat.

Emma smiled back, but almost immediately she was serious again. 'He ought to go to hospital for a check-up—and *you* ought to get dressed. Haven't you got some clothes lying around somewhere?'

He struggled to control a shiver. 'First things first.' He turned to Pete, who was still sniffing. 'There's no need for tears now, laddie, so how about mopping your face and making yourself useful? I bet you've always wanted to dial 999, so off you go to the nearest phone and do just that. Tell the ambulancemen what's happened and they'll do the rest. Get your skates on.'

The boy sped off and the dog looked after him wistfully, and then up at his master.

'It's OK, Rex,' the man said. 'I'm going to get dressed and then do some jogging.' He turned to Emma. 'You don't mind being left with the patient? I'll be back before the ambulance gets here.'

'Don't worry—I can cope!' She smiled with secret amusement. 'Do please go and get warmed up. You're steadily turning blue.'

He laughed and went off at a run, the dog leaping round him, and Emma returned her attention to Kevin. He had opened his eyes and was staring blankly into her face. Suddenly he recognised her.

'You told us not to do it,' he said faintly. 'I wish we hadn't been so silly.'

She smiled at him and smoothed his hair back, then took her sweater off and tucked it round him. 'I don't think you're likely to do it again, love.' She went on to explain about the necessity for calling an ambulance. 'I don't expect they'll keep you long at the hospital. If you like I'll ring your mum when I get home, and tell her what's happened. Will she be there?'

Kevin confirmed that she would and even managed to give Emma his phone number. Delighted that he was obviously perfectly normal, she settled down to wait patiently, with her arms folded round her body in an attempt to keep the wind at bay.

The boy, exhausted by his ordeal, had closed his eyes again, and she allowed her mind to wander back to the man who had dared to swim in the North Sea in October. She had not realised until he stood up how very tall and strong he was, with good shoulders and narrow hips, all shown off to perfection by the skimpy bright green bathing-trunks he wore. It was a long time since she had paid any attention to an attractive male figure—not since that tragic summer two years ago, when she used to swim with Paul.

He had been tall too, and as fair as the stranger

was dark, but his body had been willowy compared with this man's. For a while Emma had thought she was going to marry him, but things hadn't worked out that way. And she still didn't know why.

She sighed and thrust the unhappy past to the back of her mind—which was now its normal place—and at the same moment she heard a dog bark and saw a distant running figure.

He arrived with a flurry of shingle, greeted her with a smile and quickly checked the state of the patient.

'If you sit around any longer you'll be as blue as I was.' He removed her sweater from Kevin and substituted his own anorak. 'Do please get on with your walk and I'll take over.'

'Thanks.' She dived into the sweater and then glanced at her watch. 'I'll have to get home now. I'm nearly an hour late.'

'Do you work on Saturdays?'

'Quite often, but today I'm going to bed.' Noting his expression, she smiled. 'I've just come off night duty at the hospital.'

'So you're a nurse? I might have guessed it!' He held out his hand, taking her cold one into a warm clasp. 'I'm Craig Norbury and I've just joined the local GPs. Nice to meet you, Nurse——?'

'Emma Mayfield.'

He seemed to have forgotten to release her hand. Gently withdrawing it, she gave him another smile and began to brush the sand off her jeans.

'I expect we'll meet again before long,' Craig

said. 'In a small place like this, everybody probably knows everybody else.'

'Saxham's not that small! But we're sure to meet at the hospital—the GPs are always popping in and out. It's marvellous for the patients, having their own doctors to look after them.'

'It'll be a new experience for me.'

There had been something odd in his tone, but Emma couldn't give a name to it and she dismissed it. 'Goodbye, Dr Norbury,' she said briskly, and turned away.

'Goodbye, Nurse,' he called after her.

She waved her hand without looking back and hurried on. Before long she met Pete, returning full of importance. He reported that the ambulance would soon be arriving and asked if he could ride in it.

'You'll have to see what the ambulancemen say but I expect they'll let you.' Emma smiled and then was suddenly very serious. 'You won't ever do anything like that again, will you, Pete? You do realise it might have ended quite differently?'

He nodded, shifting his feet in embarrassment, but Emma saw the scared look in his eyes and felt fairly certain she could believe him.

Emma woke slowly. A hand on her shoulder was shaking her gently and her sleep-doped brain registered that it must be time to get up. At that moment she felt she could sleep for ever.

'Four o'clock, dear,' came her mother's voice. 'I've given you an extra half-hour because you were so late getting to bed.'

Instantly everything flashed back into Emma's mind: the two boys, the cliff-fall, Dr Norbury—to say nothing of his dog. Kevin was probably safely at home again now, but she must check before she went on duty.

'Drink your tea before it gets cold,' Ruth Mayfield urged.

She crossed the room and drew the curtains back, remaining there for a moment to gaze out. She was a slender woman, with a good figure and light brown hair similar to her daughter's but without the chestnut gleam. To a casual observer it showed no signs of grey and her skin was good.

Since Dr Mayfield, a much-loved husband and father, had been killed in a road accident in the same year as Emma's boyfriend had deserted her, life for the two left behind had tended to be rather grim. Ruth kept busy—she taught at a play-school in the mornings—and Emma devoted herself to her nursing, doing her best to convince herself that it was all she needed.

The window was open and the pounding of the sea could plainly be heard. The small, narrow house was wedged in between two larger ones in Little Back Lane, which was immediately behind the grander houses overlooking the beach. It was sheltered by them from the worst of the east coast gales and suited both the occupants very well.

Emma swung her legs out of bed and stood up. 'I'd better have a shower and then phone Mrs Blackburn——'

'Who on earth's she?'

'The mother of the boy I told you about.'

To her surprise and delight, when she rang up

it was Kevin himself who answered.

'Fine!' he said in reply to her enquiry. 'I've got one or two bruises where stones hit me, but that's all.'

'You do realise how lucky you were, don't you?'

'My mum's only told me about fifty times! She's forbidden me to go on the beach for two weeks, so I don't know what we'll do on Saturdays.'

'I expect you'll find something,' Emma said, hoping it would be something sensible.

She was not due at the hospital until nine o'clock and long before that she felt wide awake and ready for anything the night had in store. It was still fine and clear when she set out on her bicycle, and she cheerfully tackled the ride, most of which was gently uphill.

Saxham cottage hospital was about half a mile from the sea. The residential part of the town had developed on both sides of the High Street, like the veins of a leaf. There were numerous narrow lanes, like the one where the Mayfields lived, and, on the outskirts, a network of more modern houses and bungalows. The hospital stood on the highest part, overlooking everything else.

It had once been a large private house standing in its own grounds and the home of Emma's great-grandfather, a self-made man who had accumulated a fortune manufacturing agricultural implements. He had left instructions in his will that it was to be turned into a hospital so that local people would not have to travel forty miles to Heathbury, the county town. By the time the NHS took it over all the original money had been spent, and it depended a great deal on fund-raising efforts by the League of Friends.

This evening Emma rode her bicycle round to the cycle-sheds at the back—not much used now—and entered by a side door. Turning left, she reached the main hall, which still looked as though it belonged to a private house. There were gilt-framed pictures on the walls, flowers and plants in every available spot, and a few pieces of good antique furniture.

Emma ran lightly up the elegant staircase. As she reached the wide landing a woman in a plain dark blue dress with lace collar came out of one of the wards. She had grey hair and a pleasant, fresh-coloured face. Except for having no cap, she could have been the matron of an expensive nursing home of thirty years ago.

'Good evening, Emma.' She smiled a welcome. 'Everything all right?'

'Yes, thank you, Miss Lenton.'

'I hear you got involved in some excitement on the beach this morning.'

'It could have ended in tragedy,' Emma said soberly. 'If it hadn't been for Dr Norbury—and his dog—I don't think the boy could have been got out in time.'

'Dr Norbury?' The matron looked interested. 'I haven't met him yet, but Dr Roberts was here this morning and he mentioned he'd joined the group practice. He's quite young, I believe?'

'About thirty, I should think, and very tough. He was swimming when I first saw him!'

'Really?' Miss Lenton's eyebrows shot up, and then she remembered something. 'Dr Roberts told me he's come from a practice on the South

Coast, so perhaps that explains it.'

They agreed that it probably did and Emma asked if there were any special instructions for the night. There were three full-time staff nurses at the cottage hospital but only one was on duty at night, and she would be in charge of the whole hospital.

'That girl who was brought in with stomach pains last night has been quite all right all day. Dr Roberts says she can go home tomorrow if there's no recurrence, but he wants to be informed if they return, even if they're not very severe. You can't be too careful with children.'

'Does he suspect they're psychosomatic?' Emma asked.

'He hasn't said so, but I've got my own ideas on the subject.'

They exchanged smiles and Miss Lenton departed to her cottage in the grounds. It seemed possible, Emma remarked to her assistant, a married woman with three children, that they would have a quiet night.

'I hope so,' Celia Frost said frankly, 'because that means I shall be able to get on with my knitting.'

Emma went off to do her tour of the wards. There were four of these, and also a small number of private rooms, and it took a long time to work her way round because she liked to stop and talk to anyone who seemed in the mood. Gina Baines, the child with abdominal pain, was peacefully asleep and so were some of the older people

Making sure that the television sets were

properly switched off, Emma hoped that soon all her charges would settle down.

She and whoever was assisting her always took it in turns to walk round the wards every half-hour. Somebody might want a painkiller or some other medicament, or perhaps only a hot drink and a little whispered conversation. Tonight Celia did the first tour and returned after a brief disappearance, reporting that all was quiet.

And so it remained until three o'clock.

It was Emma's turn, and in the first three wards she found everything as it should have been. But in the fourth she got a shock.

It was a male ward and most of the patients were elderly and deaf. A chorus of snoring greeted her when she went in and she anticipated finding them all asleep. Shielding her torch with her hand, she went from bed to bed, checking automatically but nonetheless with care. On one side of the ward everything was in order but halfway down the other she halted in dismay.

John Wheeler's bed was empty.

He was a retired gardener who had had a hip replacement at another hospital and, since his home was in Saxham, had been sent to the cottage hospital to convalesce. He had been forbidden to get out of bed without help, but he was an independent old man and liked to look after himself. Emma's torchlight showed chaotic bed-clothes, a pillow on the floor and two slippers which looked as though they had been kicked out of the way.

He must have gone to the toilet, and it was just like him to attempt it by himself. Disapproving,

but not particularly worried, Emma went to look
for him. She saw him almost immediately. He was
lying sprawled on the floor by the wash-basins,
his stick beside him and the leg which had received
the new hip at an alarming angle.

Quickly Emma checked that there was nothing
else obviously wrong. He was breathing normally,
if rather fast, but there were no signs of a stroke.
He must have slipped, or overbalanced and
landed on the floor, knocking himself out.

Emma fetched a rug and carefully covered the
old man up, and then went off to ask Celia to
stay with him in case he came round and tried to
get up—she wouldn't put it past him!

'I thought the peace was too good to last,' Celia
said philosophically.

As soon as she had taken charge, Emma
phoned Miss Lenton. As always, the matron
answered the phone at remarkable speed and at
once instructed her to send for a doctor.

The Saxham GPs regarded the hospital as their
own, admitted and discharged patients and even
did minor operations there on those occasions
when a local anaesthetic could be used. There was
a note by the phone giving a number to ring in
case of need and Emma lost no time in doing so.

After a moment a sleepy voice said, 'Yes?' in
her ear, and she immediately knew that this wasn't
one of the doctors she was accustomed to phoning
in the middle of the night. Dr Roberts always said
'Hello' in a loud, fierce voice—though he was a
very nice man—and Dr Samantha Cox had such
a quiet voice that it was almost inaudible. Dr
Forbes had left, and so this must be Dr Norbury,

with whom she had had that adventure on the beach.

'I'm sorry to disturb you——' she began, only to be interrupted.

'Never mind the apologies. I'm sure you're not phoning to have a polite conversation. What's the trouble?'

She told him quickly and concisely, and he immediately asked if the man was conscious.

'Not when I left him. Do you want me to check?'

'No, thanks—I'll be with you in a few minutes.'

Miss Lenton arrived first, and then the doctor, looking tidy in a cream sweater over an open-necked shirt and a pair of cord trousers. He had brushed his hair but was in need of a shave. Miss Lenton looked, as always, very much the matron.

'I thought your voice was familiar,' Craig said, when Emma opened the front door, 'but I don't think I should have recognised you from your appearance.' They began to climb the stairs together. 'Now, tell me exactly what happened.'

It took only a moment, and then he asked another question.

'I'm not familiar with cottage hospitals. Is there an operating-theatre?'

'Oh, yes.' Honesty forced her to add, 'Of course it's only small, but it gets quite a lot of use. Mr Wheeler's hip was done at a specialist hospital, so I suppose he'll have to go back there, won't he?'

'It seems likely.'

They had reached the ward and Miss Lenton came forward to receive them.

'Good morning, Doctor.' She held out a formal

hand with a regal air. 'I don't think we have met before. May I welcome you to Saxham?'

Emma stole a glance at him and saw his lips twitch. He murmured something and Miss Lenton continued.

'Your patient is still lying where he fell. I thought it better we should not try to move him.'

'Quite right. I expect you can produce a trolley?'

'I already have, Doctor. I think we can get the patient on to it between us.'

'I shall want to examine him first. Has he come round?'

'Yes, but he's confused. I suspect concussion.'

They had reached the toilet annexe and Celia stood up, looking curiously at the new doctor. He gave her a courteous nod and went down on his knees. With great care and gentleness he examined the leg which had been operated on. Watching the exploring fingers, Emma felt sure her fears were about to be confirmed.

'I'm afraid we've got a fracture here,' Craig said quietly. 'I'll immobilise the limb before we try to move him.'

The old man seemed puzzled by all the people round him but made no protest. Eventually, after a lot of careful effort, he was back in bed and Emma was fitting side-boards to it, so that it would be quite impossible for him to attempt another excursion.

'I'll phone the consultant in the morning,' Craig said, 'and give you a ring to tell you what he wants at this end. It's almost certain the old chap will have to be transferred to the other hospital.'

Refusing coffee, he went downstairs with Emma to see him out. In the entrance hall he paused and looked round.

'Whoever would have thought this place was a hospital? It's just like a private house——'

'Which is what it used to be,' Emma put in. Defiantly, she added, 'Saxham people like it this way. They're not scared of coming here—it's like a holiday.'

Craig looked down at her and she felt dwarfed, although she was five feet seven, which was quite a reasonable height for a girl.

'It must be a frustrating place to nurse. There's no room for all the modern equipment which is taken for granted these days.' With his hand on the door-lock, he paused. 'Oh, well—from what I hear you won't have to put up with it much longer. Dr Roberts says this place is going to be pulled down before long and there's to be a fine new hospital on a different site. Not in Saxham, I'm afraid, but about ten miles inland, so that more people can get there easily.'

Emma stared at him aghast. Pull down the cottage hospital her great-grandfather had bequeathed to the town? It couldn't be true! A small place like Saxham often had rumours travelling round and they usually turned out to be false. This must be one of those.

And yet the story had apparently come from Dr Roberts—he wouldn't pass on anything like that unless there was a good foundation for it.

Something in Emma's face must have alerted Craig to her state of mind, for he gave her an encouraging smile. 'Just think how much you'll enjoy working somewhere really up-to-date. You won't want to go back to this antiquated old place, that's for sure.'

He tweaked a small tendril of hair, which had escaped from the pleat, and pushed it back into place. 'Goodbye for now, Emma. I'll be in touch about Mr Wheeler.'

When she had closed and locked the door, Emma leaned back against it for a moment. She couldn't remember her great-grandfather, but her grandfather and father had both been doctors, dedicated to the service of the town and its hospital. What would they have thought of this horrible idea?

They would have fought against it, she felt sure. Was there anything she could do to defend the cottage hospital?

CHAPTER TWO

GREATLY perturbed, Emma climbed the stairs. Miss Lenton was on the landing, talking to Celia, but she broke off the conversation as soon as her staff nurse appeared.

'I'm on my way back to bed now. I don't think you'll have any more trouble with Mr Wheeler now that he's been sedated. Don't disturb him in the morning. The longer he sleeps, the better. Goodnight once again—or perhaps I should say good morning?' She looked surprised as Emma began to follow her downstairs. 'Is something worrying you?'

Emma made no attempt to deny it. 'Dr Norbury just gave me an awful shock and I wondered if you'd heard anything. He says our hospital is going to be scrapped and a new one built further away. It's to be bigger, and that means less friendly, and—and everybody will hate it!'

'That's a very sweeping statement!' The matron smiled but was immediately serious again. 'As a matter of fact, Dr Roberts mentioned it last time he was here. Apparently they want to pull down the old geriatric hospital at Stonebridge and build a new one, large enough to accommodate the old people and us as well. You have to admit, Emma, that Stonebridge definitely needs replacing. It still looks just like the nineteenth-century workhouse it once was.'

'Then why can't they just build a new Stonebridge and leave us alone?' Emma demanded.

The only answer she received was a shrug, and she went slowly back upstairs, feeling that perhaps she'd made rather a fool of herself. She shouldn't have allowed her emotions to get the better of her to such an extent.

The fact remained, though, that her outburst hadn't altered the way she felt.

She was glad when the night ended and they could start the early morning routine. There was a lot to do for just two nurses, with patients varying so much, both in age and what was wrong with them. It was impossible to think about anything except the job in hand.

Gina, the ten-year-old who had had abdominal pains—now mysteriously vanished—was wide awake and eager to help with the chores. Emma allowed her to do what she could and, as the pressure eased, seized the opportunity to put out a few feelers. Apparently the child had enjoyed being in hospital and didn't want to go home.

'Daddy's not there any more,' she said with a suspicious quiver in her voice. 'He's gone to stay with another lady, and we've got an uncle in his place and I don't like him.' There was a long pause, but Emma sensed there was more to come. 'Mummy likes him, though. She kisses him, and she says I must kiss him too and I don't want to.'

'Have you got any brothers and sisters?'

'No, I wish I had, but there's only me.' Gina sighed heavily.

The day nurses were arriving and there was nothing Emma could do about the situation then, but she resolved to report the conversation to Miss Lenton and ask if counselling could be arranged.

Later on, when she went down to the beach for her usual walk, she started thinking about the proposed new hospital. Daylight had brought an improvement in her spirits and she felt a little more optimistic. Perhaps it was only a rumour after all, and she had been working herself up for nothing.

The weather was nothing like yesterday. There was a grey mist hanging over the sea and a dampness in the air, but Emma strode along with her head up, taking in deep breaths of the moist air and not caring that her hair and clothing were glistening with drops of water.

As she passed the site of yesterday's near-tragedy, the memory of it inevitably surged to the forefront of her mind. The sand at the base of the cliff was still disturbed, a poignant reminder of what had nearly happened. Wishing she hadn't been given such a vivid imagination, she hurried on, and soon rounded the cliff-fall which hid the steps from view.

Coming towards her she saw a man and a dog. The animal had his ears pricked and suddenly he began to race towards Emma, rushing up to her with a furiously wagging tail and planting two sandy paws on her jeans.

'You've remembered me!' She gave Rex a friendly rub on his dark head and picked up a piece of driftwood, which she threw inexpertly towards the sea.

'He'll be your friend for life,' said a voice.

Emma had been so absorbed in her reunion

with the dog that she had forgotten his owner. Craig was looking down at her with his hands in his pockets and a friendly smile on his face.

'Oh—er—hello,' she said weakly.

'Not a very nice morning, is it?'

'No, but it's often like this in November. I don't mind.'

There was a small pause, and then Craig said, 'I hope you didn't have any more trouble with Mr Wheeler.'

'None at all. He was still asleep when I left.'

'I'll ring the consultant when I get back to my flat. He'll probably be up by then.'

They both laughed, and suddenly Emma's tension left her. She had liked Dr Norbury yesterday, and it was ridiculous to treat him as though he was in the doghouse just because last night he had given her a most unwelcome piece of news. Besides, hadn't she now decided it might be only a rumour? And so, when he asked if she was returning by the steps, she confirmed it, and made no attempt to dodge walking home with him.

'I prefer this route back,' she confided as they toiled up to join Rex, who was waiting at the top. 'There's a lovely view in good weather, and also I've got an aged great-aunt living in one of the houses nearer the town. I like to call on her sometimes. She's ninety-two and still looks after herself.'

'Are you going to call today?'

Emma shook her head. 'I've been quite recently, and I have to be careful or she gets the idea that her independence is being threatened.'

They walked on in silence for a short while,

the dog busy hunting among the stunted gorse
bushes on their right.

'These cliffs are very high for sandy ones,' Craig
said. 'No wonder they're so dangerous. It looks
to me as though chunks frequently break off from
the top. And just look at the path—it's constantly
re-routed away from the edge.'

'I don't really like looking at the bits of the old
path which disappear into space,' Emma confided,
'So when I'm passing those spots I stare out
to sea.'

'I hope you look where you're going.' He
laughed. 'Or you might follow the old bit of path
and walk right over the edge.'

'Please——' she put out her hand involuntarily
'—don't say things like that. It scares me.'

He took her hand in his and held it warmly.
'You've obviously been cursed with an imagination that runs riot.'

'You can say that again!' She made an ineffec-
tual attempt to extricate her hand and then, rather
than make an issue of it, decided to leave it
where it was.

Before long they came to the first houses and
the path became a track.

'Which is your great-aunt's?' Craig asked. 'Is it
one of the bungalows?'

'It's further on—nearly the last one on the sea-
ward side—and it's certainly not a bungalow. It's
quite old house, flint-built and entirely unmod-
ernised, except for having an indoor toilet. She's
made up her mind she's going to die there, so I
don't know what will happen if she gets ill.'

'I've had no experience of aged relatives, but

it sounds as though they're a pain in the neck.'
He turned round to whistle his dog, who had
vanished among the bushes, and Emma seized the
opportunity to rescue her hand. 'I've hardly any
relations at all,' he went on, 'and those I have
got are scattered round the world.'

'What about your parents?'

'They live in Eastbourne but they separated as
soon as I qualified, so now I've got two homes,
neither of which is a real home.'

'Do you mind?' Emma ventured.

Craig did not immediately reply. Stealing a look
at his face, she saw that his grey eyes had an
inward look, and she guessed that he was searching for an honest answer.

But all he came up with was, 'Yes and no.'

'Meaning?'

'Exactly what I said. Most of the time I'm quite
happy with the present situation, but there are
occasions when I go all sentimental and yearn
for a proper family background. Needless to say,
Christmas is one of those.' He gave a slightly
embarrassed laugh. 'You'd think I would have
grown out of that nonsense by now.'

It was on the tip of Emma's tongue to suggest
he spend Christmas Day at her house, but she bit
it back, horrified at such impulsiveness. She'd met
the man for the first time only yesterday, and early
this morning had had quite a fierce encounter
with him.

Her brain must be suffering from night duty; it
was high time she went to bed. If this was the
way she was going to behave when in Craig's
presence, it was a good thing her spell on nights

would end next Friday and the early morning walks would cease.

Great-Aunt Mary's house had just come into view, and Emma seized the opportunity to change the subject. They were quite close to the town now and the track was more of a road, with dwellings on both sides. Square and solid, Cliff House had withstood the east coast gales for a hundred years, but in its younger days it had been fifty yards from the cliff-edge. Now it was horrifyingly close.

'Last winter, after a spell of heavy rain, a huge slice of the garden disappeared over the edge,' Emma said soberly.

'Good God! She shouldn't be living there at her age.'

'Perhaps you'd like to try and move her? She was born at that house and has lived there all her life. She never married.'

'What sort of health does she have?'

'Good, on the whole, apart from some arthritis.'

They were near the town now and about to pass Cliff House. It stood squarely in its derelict garden, facing the North Sea with, so Emma liked to imagine, an air of defiance which matched the attitude taken up by its owner.

'Is the old lady a relative on your father's side?' Craig asked.

'Yes. Her name is Mayfield, the same as mine, and she's descended from my great-grandfather.' Emma paused, and then found herself adding, 'He's the man who gave the money in his will for his house to be turned into a hospital.'

'So the hospital is a family affair?' he exclaimed, looking down at her with interest. 'No wonder you don't want it to close. Why didn't you tell me that last night?'

Emma shrugged, trying to appear more nonchalant than she felt. 'It didn't seem to be the right time—you wanted to get home to bed and I had to get back on duty. Anyway, it's so long ago. Very few people living in Saxham now can remember my great-grandfather.'

'I suppose the town is full of your relations?'

'Heavens—no! There's only my mother and Great-Aunt Mary and me. The name will die out in the not very distant future.' A shadow crossed her face. 'With the hospital gone too, we'll all be forgotten.'

They had come to the end of the cliff road, and Emma had only to cross the High Street and she would be nearly home. As she paused on the kerb, Craig put his hands on her shoulders. Startled, she glanced up, her hazel-green eyes apprehensive.

'I really do understand your feelings about the future of the hospital, but that doesn't mean I go along with them. You can't make the clock stand still, you know, especially in medicine. There's got to be change and progress, and that means an up-to-date building to accomodate the new technology and people trained to use it. As it stands, the cottage hospital is not much more than a glorified convalescent home.'

Emma's face was scarlet and her eyes blazed. 'How dare you call it that?' She wrenched her shoulders free. 'There are lots of people in Saxham who would have died if the hospital hadn't nursed them back to health. There's even a casualty department and——'

'OK! OK!' He held up his hand to stop the flow. 'I'm sure everything you've just said is perfectly true, but it doesn't alter my opinion one little bit——'

'I never thought it would.' Emma had regained her control, but she was still angry. 'It's probably impossible for a stranger to appreciate how local people feel on such a subject, but when you've been here a little longer maybe you'll find out. In the meantime we shall have to agree to differ.' Or avoid each other altogether, but it didn't seem likely that would be possible.

Walking up Little Back Lane, she was further annoyed to find herself still thinking about the new doctor. He had mentioned a flat, but she had no idea of its whereabouts or whether he lived there alone with the dog. If he was married, he would surely have referred to his wife by now.

Very likely he had a small flat and a daily woman, who cleaned for him and perhaps did a bit of cooking, or he might have his main meal out. With the uncertain hours that doctors kept, that would probably be the best solution.

Emma's wandering thoughts stopped with a jerk as she reached the gate into their minute front garden. What on earth was she thinking of, to let her mind dwell on anything as unimportant as Dr Norbury's living conditions? They would be revealed eventually, and for the present she would have no difficulty in getting along without the information.

Laughing at herself, Emma went up the path and into the house.

The following morning it was raining, and she had no difficulty in forgoing her walk. The rain continued for two days, and suddenly it was the middle of the week and her period of night duty was nearly over.

There had been no more drama after Mr Wheeler had fallen in the toilet annexe. His consultant had summoned him back to the hospital where he had had his hip replacement, and his bed was occupied by a younger man with severe bronchitis. He was a patient of Dr Roberts, and late one evening Emma caught the doctor there and managed to talk to him about Gina.

Stout and stocky, with small bright eyes which normally twinkled cheerfully, he listened gravely to what she had to say.

'I had a superficial knowledge of the child's home circumstances,' he said, 'but not of her feelings about them. Thank you, Emma, for drawing my attention to the way she has reacted to the new man in her life.'

'I just thought it might be the cause of the pains.'

'It's certainly a possibility.' He produced a small scribbling-pad and wrote something on it. 'The matter will have to be handled extremely tactfully but I'll see what can be done.' He peered at Emma over his half-glasses. 'You're looking a bit peaky, my dear. Have you nearly finished on nights?'

'I don't feel peaky,' she protested. 'But I'm quite glad that Friday will be my last night on duty for a while. It's great to be able to look forward to three days' holiday before starting work again.'

'That reminds me. My wife and I are giving a drinks party on Sunday at twelve noon. We'd both be delighted if you and your mother would come. It's to welcome our new partner into the practice and introduce him to some of the local worthies. Have you met him yet?'

'Oh, yes. I had to call him out in the middle of the night.' She hesitated, and decided to say nothing about their other meetings. 'My mother doesn't know him, of course.'

'We shall look forward to seeing you both.' Dr Roberts beamed at her and went on his way.

Emma would have liked to ask him about the future of the hospital, but he was obviously in a hurry. By now she had almost convinced herself that the awful news given her by Craig was nothing but another rumour, but it would have been nice to hear a senior doctor's opinion.

Friday came and Emma struggled out of bed to prepare for her last night. A short time later, showered and wearing her dark blue uniform dress, she went downstairs to supper.

The small cottage had no dining-room, but the kitchen was big enough to include a dining-annexe and they usually ate their main meal in there. Ruth was sitting at the table with the local weekly paper spread out and she appeared strangely absorbed in it.

'Anything interesting?' Emma asked, looking over her shoulder.

Ruth glanced up. 'I don't think interesting is

quite the right word—alarming would be more suitable.'

Emma's heart turned over and an awful premonition seized her. 'What do you mean?'

'There's a piece here about the hospital. It's been announced by the Chief Executive of the Health Services Trust that Saxham cottage hospital and the geriatric hospital at Stonebridge are both to be scrapped, and a grand new building—a much larger one—is to be erected on a site still to be chosen.' Ruth turned round and looked into her daughter's appalled face. 'Oh, Emma—whatever would your father have said?'

They both knew the answer to that but Emma ignored the question. The time had come to admit that she had known for several days that this might be going to happen.

'However did you manage to keep it to yourself?' her mother asked, when she had been told the full story.

'By kidding myself it might be only another rumour,' Emma said bitterly. 'I still don't quite understand how two doctors knew about it beforehand.'

'I don't see much difficulty there. There was probably a leak—there usually is with decisions of that sort. It doesn't really matter anyway—it's been confirmed now, and I suppose we shall have to come to terms with it. If we can.'

Emma took a few agitated steps across the room and leaned against the Aga, which had been their one extravagance when they moved to Little Back Lane. There were times when its comforting warmth on her back made her feel great, but tonight she was unaware of it.

'I expect it will be the chief topic of conversation at the party on Sunday,' Ruth went on. 'Everybody takes the *Courier* in Saxham so they'll know about it.'

'They'll all be absolutely livid,' Emma said confidently.

To her surprise, her mother hesitated.

'All the older people will be,' she agreed eventually, 'but I'm not so sure about the newcomers. I have an uneasy feeling they won't be interested, except perhaps those who've actually used the hospital.'

Emma looked disbelieving, but made no comment and sat down at the supper table. She and her mother often disagreed about small things. It was unusual to do so over anything of such huge importance as the future of their beloved hospital.

Dr Roberts' house was in an unmade-up private road near the hospital. He and his wife, a motherly type of woman rapidly turning grey and doing nothing to hide it, had invited about forty people to meet the new doctor and there were cars parked all along the road. It was a fine morning and Emma and Ruth arrived on foot. Since Dr Mayfield's death they had not been able to afford a car.

As they walked up the drive they met a tall young woman hurrying down. Dr Samantha Cox was in her late twenties. She nearly always wore trousers—though on this occasion she was clad in a plain grey suit—and her blonde hair hung dead straight on both sides of a very attractive face.

Her chief interest, apart from her work, was golf.

'Babies really are the most inconsiderate little creatures!' she exclaimed ruefully, but with a smile not far away. 'One of my expectant mums has gone into labour and her panic-stricken husband has rushed her to hospital. I don't suppose it's in the least urgent, but it's a first baby and I have to go and check.'

'It's a shame you'll miss most of the party,' Emma said.

'A doctor's life is made up of misses like that. In this case, it's not only that Mrs Stapleton is a patient of mine but I'm on call as well. Somebody had to be, and I was the obvious person. It wouldn't have done to have had the host or the guest of honour rushing off. Cheerio!'

'Nice girl,' Ruth said as they approached the front door. 'We're lucky in our doctors in Saxham.'

'You don't know anything about the new one.'

'No, but you've met him, and I haven't heard you say anything against him.'

Emma debated whether to confess that her feelings towards Dr Norbury were distinctly ambivalent. Sometimes she liked him—up to a point—but at others he infuriated her—like when he sided with the powers-that-be who wanted to pull the hospital down.

It was obviously neither the time nor the place. The door was being opened by an unseen hand and the noise of the party rushed out to greet them.

People were spilling out of the large drawing-room, which ran from front to back of the house,

and the Mayfields eased their way in to find their
hosts. Craig was the centre of a group made up,
on the whole, of youngish people. He was very
well turned out, in a casual suit of fine tweed
worn with a white silk shirt and his hospital tie.
His hair had obviously recently been tended by a
barber and clung neatly to his head with a very
slight suggestion of a wave.

'He's very good-looking,' Ruth murmured in
her daughter's ear. 'Married?'

'I don't think so.'

'Then he ought to be. A young doctor with
looks like that should always be married. It's a
sort of protection.'

'Not any more it isn't!' Emma burst out laughing. 'Really, Mum, your ideas are positively
archaic at times.'

Ruth was unperturbed. She had heard it all
before and she merely smiled.

Craig had noticed them both and he reached
out a hand towards them, smiling a welcome.

'This is my mother.' Emma urged her forward and watched him produce his most
charming smile.

She felt detached and slightly cynical as the
two exchanged formal greetings, and then scolded
herself for feeling like that. This was a party and
Craig was supposed to be the centre of it. He was
merely playing the role allotted to him by the
senior partner.

Soon Ruth managed to slip away and Emma
lost sight of her, but there was no chance of
making her own escape because Craig was still
talking to her.

'When do you start on day duty?' he asked, making it sound as though he really wanted to know.

'On Tuesday. We always get three days off after coming off nights—that is if nothing prevents it. I have an uneasy feeling I might get summoned back tomorrow. The husband of one of the part-time staff nurses is ill and she might have to ask for a day off.'

'That's a pity from your point of view. Surely it would be better if the chap was transferred to an empty bed in the hospital, then she could look after him and perform her duties as well.' Craig raised his eyebrows and gave Emma a slightly twisted smile.

'That would be ridiculous!' Emma bit her lip and controlled herself. 'We may be informal at the cottage hospital but we don't go as far as that.'

'I was only teasing,' Craig said softly.

She was annoyed to find herself colouring, and she managed to slip away and lose herself in the crowd.

'Let me get you another drink, Emma.' Dr Roberts had discovered her. 'What will you have?'

One glass of wine was enough for her in the middle of the day and she asked for apple juice. Returning with it, her host commented on Samantha Cox having been called away.

'I hope no more emergencies crop up or we shall lose the guest of honour, but at least he's been here long enough to have a word with nearly everybody.'

'Two crises on a Sunday in Saxham would be most unusual.'

The doctor nodded agreement and they parted. Emma began to circulate, pausing here and there to chat to people. Since she knew nearly everyone there, she had no difficulty in finding something to talk about.

Her mother found her eventually and suggested it was time to leave, but other people had had the same idea and it took some time to get near their hosts to say goodbye. As they awaited their turn, Emma heard a phone ringing somewhere in the house but thought nothing of it.

Some minutes later they got as far as the garden. As Ruth paused to admire a clump of winter heathers, Craig burst out of the front door.

'Hang on a minute, Emma!' he called.

She stopped, looking back. 'What is it?'

'Another emergency—believe it or not.' He reached her side. 'Are you desperate to get home to your Sunday lunch? Because, if not, I'd be glad if you'd come with me. It sounds as though I may need some help.'

There were two practice nurses, who worked alternately, but they were never called out on a Sunday. Besides, an emergency meant precisely that—no time to waste.

'Of course I'll come,' Emma said. 'What's happened?'

CHAPTER THREE

'MY CAR'S round the back.' Without pausing to give Emma an explanation, Craig went rushing off in that direction.

Ruth, who had heard it all, said calmly, 'I won't wait lunch for you, dear. See you some time!' With a wave of her hand, she continued down the drive.

A red BMW whirled into view and Craig leaned across to open the passenger's door. By the time Emma had fastened her seatbelt, they were half-way down the road.

'Where are we going?' she asked.

'I'm hoping you can tell me that. It's a house-boat, moored on the River Wick. Convey anything to you?'

'Oh, yes. The easiest way is to go down the High Street and turn left up on to the cliff track. There's a road branching off that which keeps close to the coast and after about half a mile it comes down to sea level. That's the mouth of the Wick. The houseboats are upstream a short distance. What exactly is the emergency?'

'A severe cut with a lot of bleeding.'

'Would that be Michael Hammond?'

Craig glanced at her in surprise. 'How did you guess?'

'He's a wood-carver—makes the most beautiful birds and colours them exquisitely. He's cut himself before but this sounds worse than usual.'

'I'm afraid you may be right.' He changed gear as they left the High Street behind and climbed up to the cliff-top. 'What worries me is that he suddenly stopped speaking after he'd given his address but he didn't hang up. Does he live alone?'

'His wife is there sometimes, but I don't think she cares much about life on a boat.'

'Can't say I blame her.'

'Mike's is beautiful—every mod-con.'

'All right in the summer, I suppose, but not at this time of the year.'

They were already coming down to the river-mouth, where there was a small marina. The dinghy-park was crowded with boats laid up for the winter, and there were a few larger ones still moored.

'We'll have to leave the car here and walk along the towpath,' Emma said.

Craig looked critically at the narrow, muddy path. 'Hellish awkward place to pick up a patient if hospitalisation should be needed.' He waved her on to lead the way.

'There are a lot worse places than this,' she reminded him over her shoulder. 'But the men manage perfectly well.'

To her surprise, Craig reacted badly to what had seemed to her a very ordinary remark.

'You can't bear to hear a single word of criticism about anything around here, can you? In your eyes the hospital is perfect, in spite of its obvious disadvantages, and now you're actually standing up for this highly dangerous towpath. I can't think why you don't pretend the cliffs are so scenically beautiful it doesn't matter that they're falling to bits.'

Emma almost halted to face him indignantly, but the thought of the waiting patient drove her on. 'I never heard such nonsense in all my life,' she told him loftily. 'I'll have it out with you later, when we've coped with Mike Hammond.'

'I shall look forward to that,' Craig said, apparently regaining his good humour.

A moment later Emma halted at a narrow gangway. Although most of the other houseboats were adorned with pot plants, or even an attempt at a tiny garden, this one was bare of such additions. The miniature deck was cluttered with various odds and ends, including a sack of coal and some logs.

She crossed it swiftly and knocked on the door. Not waiting for a reply, she pushed it open and, followed closely by Craig, went down the two steps into the studio. The long room was mostly at deck level and there were big picture windows giving a good view of the marshes on both sides of the river. Immediately it became obvious why the telephone conversation had been left unfinished.

Mike Hammond, a big man with a mass of untidy yellowish-grey hair, was lying on the floor with the phone hanging close to his head. His eyes were half-closed but he opened them wider when he became aware of their presence, and tried to speak, but the words were slurred and incomprehensible.

His left hand was bleeding freely from a cut on the palm.

Suddenly within Emma's mind a memory stirred, and she turned to Craig. 'I believe I can remember hearing he's a diabetic. It looks to me as though he's on the verge of slipping into a coma.'

'It certainly does.' Ignoring the bleeding, Craig opened his medical bag. 'I've got some glucose in here and the sooner I get it into him the better. In the meantime, see if you can find some chocolate—or ordinary sugar will do.'

For a few minutes they were both busy. Craig prepared an injection and administered it, and Emma searched in the cupboards in the galley which opened out of the big room. There was no chocolate but she mixed sugar with a little water and spooned it into the patient's mouth. He made a sound of protest but obediently swallowed.

The effect was magical. Although he still looked dazed, his words were clearer when he murmured, 'I'm afraid I've been rather a fool.' He also made an attempt to sit up, which was promptly frustrated by Craig's hand on his shoulder.

'Just lie still, Mr Hammond, and leave everything to us. I expect you realise you nearly went into a diabetic coma, but we got here in time. You must still be feeling pretty rough so I'm going to call an ambulance and get you taken to hospital. Your insulin can be checked, and also it will be much easier to deal with that cut there, though it needs a temporary bandage.'

This time the patient did not attempt a protest,

and Craig picked up the phone and made his call.

'Shall I do the bandaging?' Emma asked, knowing that doctors were apt to be inefficient at that sort of first aid.

Craig accepted the offer with a smile, and while she was busy he studied the display of beautifully carved and painted birds at the far end of the room.

'The man's a genius,' he murmured as she passed on her way to the galley to wash her hands. 'These would make wonderful Christmas presents.'

'Do you have to buy many presents?'

'About half a dozen family ones. Add to those a few friends—maybe the total is about ten or twelve.'

'Friends' probably meant girlfriends, Emma reflected. Men didn't usually give each other presents. He was the sort of man who might have quite a lot of friends of the opposite sex, particularly if he didn't have a steady relationship with anyone. Not that she had any proof of that—it might be a detached sort of affair, with one of them in Saxham and the other in Eastbourne, or anywhere else for that matter.

A shout from the riverbank broke into her thoughts and she hurriedly finished off the temporary bandage. Although Mike Hammond was a heavy man, the paramedics made light of the slippery path to the road.

'Have you realised you'll have to drive to the hospital and continue dealing with Mr Hammond there?' Emma asked as Craig locked the door behind them. 'There's no resident doctor.'

'It had occurred to me. Do you want me to drop you off somewhere near your home, or will you come too? It might even be that you'll be needed. I don't know how well-staffed they are on a Sunday.'

Sensing criticism, she said quickly, 'There's always a staff nurse on duty, and Miss Lenton is often there too, but certainly I'll come.'

When they reached the hospital, she was immediately glad she had come. Dr Cox was still there, very much involved with a difficult birth, and the staff nurse was assisting her. Miss Lenton liked to be available to talk to visitors if they seemed to welcome it, and she was very grateful to Emma for turning up to help with the stitching of Mike Hammond's wound.

In the treatment-room, she covered her leaf-green jersey party dress with a polythene apron and joined Craig, who was scrubbing up. The patient was lying propped up on the examinatioin couch and, although he looked much better, Emma noted that the experience had shaken him badly. He was soaked in sweat and shivering, but he managed to offer an apology.

'Sorry I was such a fool. I got deeply absorbed in my work and forgot about my wretched diabetes. It was after I started to feel odd that I cut myself, but my brain was so confused I could only think of ringing up a doctor. I never even thought of eating something sweet.'

Craig made no comment. Emma smiled at the repentant carver and began to put things ready for stitching. A short time later the patient was installed in one of the wards, where he would be tested to make sure his regular injection of insulin was correct.

Emma glanced at her watch. It was half-past two.

'Feeling hungry?' Craig asked.

'I haven't been thinking about it but—well, yes, I believe I am.'

'There's absolutely no doubt in my mind about the state of my own stomach. It's long ago forgotten all the bits and pieces we had at the party, and is now in the market for roast beef, Yorkshire pud and two veg. Where shall we go?'

Startled, Emma turned her head and stared at him. 'I'm going home.'

'Your mother won't be expecting you now.'

'How do you know she won't?'

'Masculine intuition.'

'There's no such thing.'

'Who cares? The fact remains that I'm inviting you to lunch with me and your reception of the invitation is most unflattering.' They were standing by his car and he took a step nearer, gazing down into her face. 'Please come, Emma. Maybe we can recapture some of the party atmosphere which was interrupted by a careless diabetic.'

Emma thought it most unlikely. Party atmosphere was a subtle thing, not to be deliberately sought. Before the accident which had resulted in her father's tragic death, she had had a lot of fun—at first with a crowd of friends and then mostly in Paul's company. Immediately after the loss of both of them, life had been grim indeed. Dr Mayfield, a good doctor and a charming man, had been financially incompetent, and the debts he had left behind him had horrified his widow and daughter. They had had to move from a large, comfortable house to Little Back Lane; giving up the car had only been one of their sacrifices.

'I'm getting hungrier by the minute,' Craig said plaintively. 'Are you coming or not?'

Emma made up her mind. 'Yes, please, but I must ring my mother first.'

'I thought we'd dealt with all that,' he complained.

'It's just to tell her not to go on keeping my lunch hot.'

With a martyred expression, he offered her his car-phone, and she made the call.

'You'll have to choose where we eat,' he said as he drove down the road. 'I haven't been here long enough to learn anything about the local places.'

They went to the Hungry Dolphin, a popular pub on the front, and found it now only half-full. For a while they both ate hungrily, not talking very much, and then Craig laid down his knife and fork and looked straight at Emma.

'Now tell me about yourself.'

Astonished, she met his eyes across the table. They were lively and full of interested enquiry. 'Why should I?' she demanded.

'Because I want to know. What better reason could there be?'

That defeated her and she said hurriedly, 'You know I'm a staff nurse at the hospital and I live with my mother.'

'Brothers and sisters?'

'I have a brother in Australia who's married

and has three children, the youngest of whom we've never seen. He came over when my father died but we haven't met since.'

Craig's gaze softened. 'That must have been a very traumatic time for you and your mother. It was a car crash, wasn't it?'

'Yes.' Emma hesitated as she suddenly realised that she actually wanted to talk about that awful time. She couldn't remember ever feeling like that before. She had battened down her memories for too long, afraid of boring people and dreading not being able to control her emotions.

'He was driving back from London, where he'd been to a medical conference, and there was a head-on collision—' She broke off but Craig seemed to sense that there was more to come and waited silently. 'Both drivers were killed, and afterwards there was an enquiry, and—and the police blamed my father.'

Vaguely she became aware that Craig had put his hand over hers where it lay on the table, but she was back in the past, reliving the tragedy. It had been a long time before she and her mother had begun to pick up the pieces and rebuild their lives. In her own mind she didn't think Ruth would ever completely recover from the loss of a much-loved husband in such circumstances.

'I'd never met your mother until this morning, and then it was only for a moment,' Craig said, 'but even in that short time I sensed something about her I can't exactly describe. Would it be a sort of withdrawal?'

'That's quite a good name for it, but she was never very fond of parties.'

'How about you? Do you like them?'

Emma hesitated. She had very nearly said, I used to, but she bit it back. Instead, she said evasively, 'I don't go to very many.'

'Why not?'

Again she knew the answer, without having any intention of explaining why she had dropped out of the social round. Craig knew nothing about Paul and she wasn't about to tell him either.

With a swift movement she disengaged her hand. 'I really think it's time this inquisition stopped!'

'One more question,' he said calmly. 'What do you do when you're not working at the hospital or walking on the beach communing with the sea?'

'I do all sorts of things, just like everyone else, but I haven't got any special interests. I don't belong to the local dramatic society, or work out at the leisure centre every time I'm off duty.'

'I went there on my day off. It's quite good for a small town like this.'

Not long ago Emma would at once have accused him of being patronising, but now she merely raised her eyebrows and gave him a half-smile, which he immediately interpreted correctly.

'Saxham *is* a small town—you can't deny it.'

'I've no intention of trying. Would you like some more coffee?'

The pub had supplied them with a large pot of strong black coffee and cream to go with it. They had been gradually working their way down it as they talked. As Craig held out his cup, Emma took charge of the conversation.

'We've talked about me long enough, so how

about doling out a little information about yourself? If you've always lived on the south coast, what on earth made you come to East Anglia?'

'Several reasons. For one thing I thought that, geographically, I'd like a complete change and I chose this part of the country because Sammy Cox is here.' Seeing Emma's look of surprise, he went on casually, 'I've known her for years. We trained together at the London Hospital and have always kept in touch. She's good fun if you can keep her off the subject of golf.'

'So you think you made the right decision?'

'I'm fairly sure, but I wish the summer was before us instead of winter. I'm more at home on a Mediterranean beach with a few odd palm trees in the background than I am on a shingle beach with crumbling cliffs and an east wind.'

'I'm not,' Emma said emphatically. 'I love the wildness of a winter sea, with the gulls screaming over the tossing waves and the wind in my hair and——' She broke off. 'Sorry—I got a bit carried away. Actually, I've gone off hot, sunny beaches since they started warning us against lying in the sun too much because of skin cancer. It bothers me to see people taking risks of that sort.'

They were silent for a moment and then Craig said, 'Rex likes it here anyway, and I expect I'll get used to it.'

'What have you done with him today?'

'We had our usual early walk, and then I left him at my flat. I'm lucky enough to have what they call a garden flat and, what's more, it's a walled garden, and I've fixed things so he can go in and out as he pleases.'

'He's a very lucky animal.'

'That's what I tell him. Incidentally, he's about ready for another walk, so how do you think he'd like to have a double escort?'

'I shouldn't think he'd care one way or the other.' Emma bent to retrieve her handbag from the floor. 'Thank you for the gorgeous meal—I don't think I shall want anything else to eat today.'

'You don't feel you ought to walk it off?'

She shook her head. 'What I feel I ought to do is go straight home. My mother will wonder where I've got to.' Guessing that he was going to offer her a lift, she held up her hand. 'It's not far from here, but at least I shall get a little of that exercise you seem to think I need. Have a good walk— and give my love to Rex.'

There was a narrow cut-through to Little Back Lane. As she left the sea-front, Emma glanced back, and noted how the pale winter sunshine was turning the waves to gold. It would have been lovely on the beach.

That evening she received the half-expected telephone call from Miss Lenton, summoning her to return to duty in the morning instead of on Tuesday.

'I'm so sorry, Emma, but I'll make it up to you at the first opportunity. I couldn't refuse to let Janet Williams have the day off to nurse her husband. He's got a very nasty bout of flu. Of course, at one time that sort of thing would have been unheard of. Nothing but a nurse's own illness could secure her a day off, but things are different now. I'm not sure I like it, but I expect I'm old-fashioned.'

Emma didn't really mind night duty but it was great to be back on days. Pedalling up the gently sloping High Street towards the higher part of the town, she wondered what the day had in store. It was some time since they had had a maternity case, and Dr Cox's patient would presumably still be there, installed in one of the single rooms.

'We've had such a quiet night, it was actually boring,' Maggie Dereham, a cheerful dark-haired girl, said with a smile. 'That baby Dr Cox delivered yesterday slept peacefully and so did her mum, but that was because she was exhausted. She had a very bad time.'

'Is she OK this morning?'

Maggie shrugged. 'It's hard to tell, but I expect you'll find out in due course. Physically she's not too bad.'

Emma was puzzled but asked no questions. As she had just been reminded, she would soon discover for herself how Mrs Stapleton was feeling.

'I'll help with breakfasts before I go and see her. Are you just off?'

'I sure am. My eyelids are propped up with matchsticks. You know how it is the first few nights.' Maggie yawned widely. 'What's the outside world like?'

'Dull but dry. May rain later.'

'It can do what it likes as long as I'm asleep. Cheerio—have a nice day!'

Emma went into the first ward, where she found

a nurse dishing out breakfasts from a big trolley. The patients were all sitting up, looking cheerful and expectant, and she had a word with each of them as she helped to hand out their meal.

The wards at the cottage hospital were old-fashioned, with two rows of beds facing each other. Quite a lot of the patients liked it that way, considering it more friendly; it certainly made things much easier for the nurses.

Remembering Maggie's slightly mysterious concern for the new mother, Emma prepared her breakfast tray herself and took it in. There were four single rooms, opening out of their own corridor, and they were used for the occasional private patient as well as maternity cases and, sometimes anyone who was too ill to be nursed in a public ward. This morning Anne Stapleton's room was the only one occupied.

'Good morning, Mrs Stapleton.' Smiling cheerfully, Emma pulled the bed-table into position with one hand, and at the same time glanced at the baby. She was glad to see she was still fast asleep.

Anne was propped up in bed, and for a moment she continued to stare into space. Emma had an impression of pale hair, pale face and two large pale blue eyes. She looked nothing like a radiant mother who had successfully produced her first child, but she did manage to murmur an almost inaudible reply to the greeting.

Ignoring it all, Emma walked round the bed to take a proper look at the infant. She saw a small puckered face and a blob of a nose, the whole crowned by tufts of darkish hair.

'You've got a lovely baby! Have you chosen a name for her yet?'

There was a long silence and then a muttered reply. 'We only chose boys' names. Somehow we felt quite sure that was what I was going to have.'

So that was the trouble. The child was the wrong sex.

Emma was not seriously concerned because it happened so often. Even though it had for some time been possible to find out the sex of the foetus, a lot of parents didn't bother, or didn't approve. In most cases their initial disappointment soon turned to pleasure in the possession of a healthy baby. No doubt the Stapletons would be the same.

Anne seemed to have revived a little, though she was taking no interest in her breakfast. Emma poured her a cup of tea and, sensing she was ready to talk, sat down on the edge of the bed

'Actually,' Anne confided, 'I don't mind so very much that we've got a daughter, but my husband was really upset. He belongs to an old family and we've got a place in the country. Most of the land has been sold but we've managed to keep the house going, so it's still important to have an heir. I—I feel I've failed him.' Her voice quivered ominously.

Emma took one of her hands and held it firmly. 'Listen, Anne, the sex of the baby has nothing to do with you, so you can put that idea out of your head right away. This is your first child, isn't it? Then you've got plenty of time to try again.'

'I'm thirty next birthday.'

'So what? Age isn't nearly as important as it

used to be, and couples quite often put off beginning a family until they feel they can cope. Drink your tea, love, and start looking forward to your husband's first visit. He is coming today?'

'He said so last night, but it won't be until the afternoon.'

'That will give you time to have a good rest. I expect you're worn out after the long labour you had yesterday, and that's probably why you've been taking your husband's attitude so seriously. Most men want to have a son for their first child but they soon get used to having a daughter instead.'

Anne made no comment, but Emma was glad to see she was looking brighter. Leaving her to get on with her breakfast, she went off in search of Miss Lenton, to whom she gave a full account of her conversation with the new mother.

'I hope she's not heading for post-natal depression,' the matron said anxiously. 'It's such a pity when that happens, at a time when a woman should be feeling particularly happy.'

'I don't think so—not in the sense you mean— though she was certainly depressed. She has good reason if her husband is as disappointed as she seems to imagine.'

'We must hope the tiresome man has now got over it—or at least will have enough sense to hide it from his wife.'

It was time for the after-breakfast medicine round and Emma went to fetch the trolley and unlock the drugs cupboard. It took her a long time to work her way round the four wards because, as always, she stopped to talk to most of the forty patients. They were all adults at present, even in the ward which was normally reserved for children, a state of affairs which was unlikely to last long.

After that she supervised Mrs Stapleton's first attempt to feed her baby, and explained the importance of the milky fluid which was all she would have to offer the child for a day or two.

'It's called colostrum, and it's very important that the child should have it. Besides, it gets the infant used to sucking, and she'll know what to do when your proper milk arrives.'

The new mother listened intently and Emma was glad to note that she was looking better. All that was needed now was for Mr Stapleton to turn up as promised, and in a more reasonable frame of mind, and all would be well.

A multitude of jobs filled up what remained of the morning. The great variety of her work at the cottage hospital was the main reason Emma loved nursing there. Medical and surgical cases were likely to be found in the same ward, though they tried to keep fracture patients together, particularly if they were young motorcycle enthusiasts.

She ate her lunch in the dining-room on the ground floor. It was next to the annexe at the back, which contained the day centre for local pensioners, and the same kitchen served both. The food was good and much enjoyed by the elderly people of Saxham who needed such facilities.

What would happen to them if the hospital was scrapped?

Brooding over it, Emma scarcely noticed what

she was eating. It was three days now since the closure had been confirmed in the local paper, and she hadn't even begun to think what to do, nor had she made any attempt to enlist helpers. Could one nurse fight the local Health Services Trust all by herself?

And how was she to set about it?

Emma went back on duty without her brain producing any brilliant ideas, and was forced to shelve the problem. She had no free time that afternoon because she was due to go home at five o'clock.

Visiting times were elastic and people began to arrive soon after the patients had finished their after-lunch nap. Emma had expected Mr Stapleton to be among the first, and when three o'clock came without any sign of him, she went along to see how his wife was coping with his absence.

She was not surprised to find her sitting rigidly upright and looking very distressed.

'Ron isn't coming—I know he's not!' she burst out.

Emma approached the bed with a sinking heart. 'It's still quite early—something must have delayed him.'

'Do you really think so?' Anne snatched at the offered straw. 'I'm so terribly afraid he's still feeling the same as he did last night.'

She wasn't the only one, but Emma hid her own doubts determinedly. 'All sorts of things could have delayed him. Besides, it probably wouldn't occur to him that you'd be sitting here as taut as a tennis racquet waiting for him to appear!' She glanced round the room. 'Have you got any clothes here?'

'Only the awful maternity gear I was wearing yesterday.'

'Well, you certainly won't want to wear that, but I do think you ought to get up and sit in your armchair.' She picked up a pretty black and peacock-blue caftan. 'Put this on and brush your hair and do your face, and he'll be here by the time you've finished.'

She helped her out of bed and left her to carry out the instructions, hoping fervently that Ron Stapleton wouldn't let her down.

There was a man coming up the stairs when she reached the landing, but it wasn't a stranger. It was Dr Norbury.

CHAPTER FOUR

CRAIG was looking rather at a loss and he greeted Emma with relief. 'Hi! I was wondering which way to go.'

'Who do you want to see?'

'That maternity case. Sammy Cox is off duty today and she asked me if I would look in. She seems a bit concerned about Mrs Stapleton, but she was hurrying off to play golf and didn't go into details. I got the impression it's a gut feeling she has, rather than anything specific.'

'It was a difficult birth and she's very tired, but there's also another problem. They wanted a boy—at least her husband did—and they've got a girl.'

'He'll soon get over the disappointment,' Craig said easily.

'That's what I tried to tell her, and she cheered up a bit, but I think she's still worried.'

'Hasn't Mr Stapleton been to see her today?'

'Not yet.' Emma lowered her voice. 'I'm beginning to take a dislike to that man and I've never even seen him.'

She had kept Craig talking deliberately, so that Anne would have time to tidy herself, thereby— she hoped—boosting her morale a little, but she couldn't hold him up any longer, and consequently she led the way to the single rooms.

'The baby's OK,' she went on, 'and physically

her mum is too, except, as I said, for being so tired.'

'I think you're worrying yourself about nothing,' he said firmly. 'I haven't done a lot of midwifery, but it seems to me quite natural for a woman to feel low after a difficult birth. She's probably convinced she couldn't bear to go through all that ever again, and that her husband will certainly want her to, since the child's the wrong sex.'

Put like that, it made sense, and Emma flashed him a smile over her shoulder. They had now reached the door of Anne's room, and as she pushed it open she couldn't fail to see the eager look of anticipation when Anne realised there was a man behind the nurse.

But it was the wrong man, and she looked at him blankly, obviously wondering who he was but not caring in the slightest.

'Hello, Mrs Stapleton.' Craig came forward with a smile, not waiting to be introduced. He explained about being asked to call by his partner but gave no hint about her concern, and then he admired the baby and examined the chart hooked on the end of the bed.

'Everything seems very satisfactory,' he observed.

'Satisfactory!' Anne, who had been keeping her emotions under tight control, startled them by bursting into tears.

Emma went up to her and knelt down beside the chair. 'My dear—you mustn't upset yourself like this—I'm sure there's no need——'

'No need?' Drowned blue eyes gazed at her

with bitter reproach. 'How can you say that after what I told you this morning? Ron's not coming— it's as simple as that—he can't forgive me for not having a boy——' A fresh outburst overwhelmed her.

Emma put both arms round her and held her tightly. From behind, Craig proffered a box of tissues. Eventually the storm subsided, though Anne was still catching her breath like a child and her face, which she had fortunately not had time to make up, was blotched and swollen.

'The best thing you can do,' Craig said quietly, 'is ring up your home and find out if anything has delayed your husband. There could be several quite ordinary reasons for his not getting here yet. Nurse will bring you the mobile phone and you can get on with it right away.'

The effect on Anne was miraculous. 'What a good idea!' She scrubbed away the last of her tears and looked up at Emma. 'Could you——?'

'There's just one thing. If Mr Stapleton is— er—not in the house, will there be anybody to answer the phone?'

'Probably. We have a married couple, and they take their free time mostly in the evenings, after we've had an early dinner, but they do go out sometimes after lunch. The arrangement is very free and easy.'

It sounded a well-off household, Emma reflected as she went to fetch the phone, and they obviously had a great deal to be thankful for. What a pity the safe arrival of a beautiful baby hadn't been a matter for rejoicing.

While Anne made her call, she retired to the

corridor with Craig. They stood close together in the narrow space, just out of earshot. He was leaning against the wall, his arms folded, and staring down at his feet, and Emma found herself studying the inordinate length of his lashes, which she couldn't remember having noticed before. Thick, black and slightly curling, they hovered just above his lean, tanned cheek and entirely hid his eyes from her view.

But quite suddenly they flew up, and before she could do anything about it she was staring into a pair of enquiring grey eyes.

'You've got a very odd look on your face, Emma.' He gave her a half-smile. 'Didn't I shave properly this morning?'

Hot colour was dyeing her cheeks, but she managed to answer with a smile, 'Was I staring at you? I didn't mean to. I was wondering whether Anne's found out what's happened to her husband.'

'I should think we might peep in now and see if she's still talking,' Craig suggested.

Emma led the way, and as soon as she reached the door the silence within struck her. Anne was lying back in her chair with a despairing expression on her face.

'No luck?' Emma asked.

'He wasn't there.' Her voice was tragic.

'Then I expect he's on his way here,' Craig said confidently.

'Did you speak to someone?' Emma put in.

'Just for a minute. The Newmans were off for a drive but she told me my husband went out immediately after lunch.'

'There you are, then!' Craig exclaimed triumphantly. 'He's on his way here, like I said.'

But Anne shook her head. 'It's only three miles from Pember Hall to the hospital. It would take him about ten minutes.'

There seemed no answer to that, but Emma did her best. 'I'm quite sure there's a reasonable explanation for what seems like a mystery just at present. Please do your best not to worry, because it may upset the baby and we don't want that to happen. She's been wonderfully contented so far.'

Once outside the door, she looked up at Craig. 'I do hope the wretched man turns up soon! I've just about run out of soothing remarks, and they're not doing much good anyway.'

'I'd like to give her a sedative, but it would affect her milk and make the infant dopey.' He looked at his watch. 'What time are you off duty?'

Surprised by the question, she told him it was five o'clock. 'I've had no time off during the day, except for lunch. Otherwise I'd be here until eight-thirty.'

'That fits in very well,' Craig said enigmatically. Seeing her look of astonishment, he relented and offered an explanation. 'It so happens that I've got a patient at Pember. It would be quite easy to call at the hall after I've seen Mr Freeman and try to get some news of the missing man.'

'You're assuming he won't have turned up here before then?'

'No, I'm not. I shall check up on that when I pick you up.'

Emma looked at him blankly. Unaccustomed to such high-handedness, she was speechless, but he took pity on her and deigned to explain.

'I'm asking you to come with me because I don't want to get lost. These country addresses are the devil to find in the dark, so will you come?'

'I do have a choice, then?' she asked, with a lift of her eyebrows.

'Of course you do—I'm not proposing to kidnap you.' He touched her shoulder lightly and an odd sensation passed over her. 'Please, Emma, give me the benefit of your local knowledge.'

Put like that, it would be ungracious to refuse, and she agreed at once, but at the same time she was conscious of a sense of disappointment. It would have been nice to be asked for the pleasure of her company.

When five o'clock came she was ready and waiting, and trying not to look as though that was what she was doing. Craig arrived only five minutes late, which was pretty good for a doctor. He drew up at the front door with a swish of tyres and Emma went down the steps to meet him.

'Well?' he asked.

'There's no news. Miss Lenton phoned the hall again but the Newmans weren't back. It's really getting serious, Craig.'

He opened the car door for her. 'How is Mrs Stapleton?'

'Sunk in apathy. She doesn't know we're going to drive out to Pember. It seemed better not to tell her.' She got in and busied herself with the seatbelt. 'Miss Lenton was wondering whether we ought to tell the police.'

'They'll certainly have to be told if the disappearance isn't cleared up soon.' He started the engine and they swept down the drive and turned into the tree-lined road. 'The trouble is Ron Stapleton is a grown man, and it's a bit soon to report him as a missing person.'

Directed by Emma, he crossed the main road and plunged into a tangle of narrow roads with misleading signposts, some of which mentioned the village they were heading for while others ignored it. Quite soon they reached their objective, a village so small that it seemed to consist of little more than two rows of cottages and a church.

'I'd never have found this without your help.' Craig drew up outside number three, Pember Hall Cottages. 'Are you coming in to see the old chap?'

'Yes, I'd like to. It's Mr Freeman, isn't it? I remember him from when he was in hospital with his bronchitis last winter. A dear old man.'

Craig's eyebrows shot up. 'You have to be joking! As far as I'm concerned, he's an obstinate old so-and-so. I tried to get him to agree to spend a few days in hospital on my last visit and he refused flatly.'

'Old people—especially real country people—tend to cling to their homes,' Emma said tolerantly. 'And his daughter comes in every day to look after him, so he gets plenty of TLC.'

'Tender loving care won't cure his chest, or provide oxygen when he's fighting for breath.'

Letting him have the last word, Emma tapped on the door, opened it and looked in. 'Hello, Mr Freeman—the doctor's come to see you. Can we come in?'

He was propped up in bed in the living-room,

where a bright fire burned. Surprised to see
Emma, he peered at her from a pair of watery
old eyes and she jogged his memory.

'I helped to look after you when you were in
hospital. Remember me? My name's Emma
Mayfield.'

'Reckon I wouldn't forget a pretty girl like you!
But I dunno what you've come for today. I don't
need no nursing, 'cept what my daughter gives
me. She's a good girl, is my Lizzie.'

'I'm not here to do anything today——'

He interrupted her, jerking his head towards
Craig, who was getting out a stethoscope. 'He
your boyfriend, then?'

It was almost certainly the heat of the fire which
was making Emma's face hot, but the look of
amusement which Craig gave her didn't help.

'You've been reading too many love stories,'
she chided the old man gently. 'This is Dr
Norbury——'

'No reason why he shouldn't be your boyfriend
as well.'

'None at all,' Craig said wickedly.

He was enjoying her embarrassment, Emma
could see that plainly, and she briskly changed
the subject. 'How are you feeling, Mr Freeman?'

'None too good,' he admitted. 'I don't reckon
that there medicine of yours does much for me.'

'You're sure you've been taking it?' Craig sat
down on the bed and studied the lined old face
while he checked the patient's pulse.

'My daughter sees to that,' he assured them.
'Very particular, Lizzie is.' A twinkle came into
his eyes. 'I wouldn't be above missing a dose or

two if it was left to me. It don't taste all that good.'

In spite of Mr Freeman's derogatory remarks, Craig wrote out a repeat prescription, and they said goodbye.

'Now show me the way to Pember Hall,' he said as they got in the car.

'You just keep on past the church and take the lane beside it. It's no distance.'

While they had been talking to the old man, it had been easy to push Ron Stapleton's mysterious disappearance to the back of their minds. It was different now, and the short drive was accomplished in a taut silence. They came to wrought-iron gates standing open, and crossed a noisy cattle-grid. The dimly seen white shapes of sheep went racing off into the distance.

On both sides, just visible in the light of a youthful moon, the rough grass was broken up here and there by clumps of trees. At a little distance a small river glinted faintly, but everything else was lost in darkness.

'Is that the river which comes out near Saxham—where Michael Hammond has his houseboat?' Craig asked.

'I think so, but I've only been in these grounds once before, and that was when the Stapletons lent the park for a British Legion fête a few years ago.'

Her father had been alive then and they had attended the fête as a family, happy and relaxed on a sunny afternoon, all unaware of the tragedy which was to overtake them before long.

'Is the house a stately home?'

'Not really,' Emma said. 'It's quite modest but

very lovely, and the park's not very extensive either.'

Pember Hall came into view as she spoke—a Georgian building with a porch supported on pillars, and steps up to the massive front door. Long windows lined the front on two floors, with smaller ones above, showing lights here and there. Parked at the side of a wide turning circle there was a mud-splashed Land Rover.

'Perhaps that's Mr Stapleton's car,' Emma exclaimed excitedly.

'Could be, but at least it suggests there's someone at home. Come on—let's try the front door.'

Their ring at the bell was answered after a long wait. A short, dark-haired woman in outdoor clothing stood there, staring at them. She was breathing hard, as though she had run from the back of the house to the front. This must be Mrs Newman.

'Yes, what is it?' she asked sharply.

Craig said calmly, 'Can we see Mr Stapleton, please?'

The question seemed to increase her agitation. 'No, I'm sorry you can't. He's—he's not at home.'

She was clearly hoping they would accept the information and go away. She even began to close the door, but Craig hastily prevented the move by suggesting he and Emma should enter.

'We're from Saxham hospital,' he explained. 'This is Staff Nurse Mayfield and I'm Dr Norbury. Mrs Stapleton, as of course you know, had a baby yesterday, and she was expecting her husband to visit her this afternoon, but——'

He was interrupted by the woman suddenly flinging the door wide. 'Please, do come in. We're dreadfully worried—my husband and me—we don't know where Mr Stapleton is.'

A moment later they were inside a wide hall with a high ceiling reaching up beyond the first floor. It had black and white tiles, and a few pieces of antique furniture were arranged round the walls. There was an enormous copper bowl of bronze chrysanthemums on a table, and the atmosphere conveyed good taste and the means to indulge it.

Mrs Newman went on speaking rapidly. 'He went out after an early lunch, telling us we wouldn't be wanted any more until the evening meal——'

'I suppose he went in his car?' Craig said.

She seemed surprised. 'Oh, no—didn't I tell you he was riding? He usually takes his horse out for some part of the day, and he was busy this morning. He said he wouldn't go far because of going to see his wife later on. That'd be by car, of course. My husband's out there now, seeing if the car's still in the garage.'

Emma was puzzled. 'But what makes you think it might be? Surely Mr Stapleton came back from his ride while you were out and——'

'But he didn't! The stable door's wide open. We came home by the back drive and saw it. There's no horse there—it's empty! Oh dear, what can have happened?' She began to cry.

Emma put her arm round the heaving shoulders. 'Don't get so upset, Mrs Newman. There may be a simple explanation——'

'Only we don't know what it is,' Craig put in grimly. 'I think we should go and talk to Mr Newman. Will you show us the way, please?'

Pulling herself together, she led the way down a passage at the back of the hall. After a short distance they came to a side door and went through it into a shrubbery.

'This is a short-cut to the stable-yard,' their guide said. 'The garages are there too.'

They soon saw her husband. Dark like his wife, and not much taller, he was standing by an open garage where a car could plainly be seen. There was stabling for four horses, but all the loose-boxes were empty and the door of one of them was open,

Mrs Newman introduced the two strangers, but before anyone could say anything they all heard a sound which froze them into a listening attitude. The clip-clop of horse's hoofs.

The animal came into view—a handsome chestnut with gleaming coat and a white blaze down his nose. He was trotting sedately, but when he saw the little group his ears pricked and he slightly increased his pace, cleverly avoiding the trailing reins.

'Oh, my God——' Mr Newman was the first to speak '—I knew there'd been an accident—all along I knew it——'

'It certainly looks like it,' Craig agreed, 'but there could be another explanation. Mr Stapleton might have dismounted for some reason and the horse escaped.'

Knowing nothing of horses, Emma made no comment. Instead she said diffidently, 'Do you think we ought to phone the police and ask them to organise a search?'

No one answered for a moment. Mr Newman had taken charge of the animal and was talking to it in a calm voice. His wife was twisting her handkerchief in her hands and looked as though she had given up. Craig had taken a quick look at his watch and she guessed he was worrying about evening surgery.

'I don't think it would be much good asking for a search,' he said eventually, 'but we could ring up and enquire if they know of any riding accidents around here. If the answer's no we must start looking ourselves.' He frowned, thinking hard. 'I'll phone Sammy—she'll have got back from her golf long ago—and see if she can take surgery for me. She knows I'd do the same for her.'

The phone calls were soon made, and by the time Craig reappeared the horse had been unsaddled and shut in the loose-box.

'He ought to be rubbed down,' Mr Newman said in a worried voice. 'Mr Stapleton's very particular about that.'

'I think finding his owner is even more important. Put a rug over him and bring one with you in case it's needed. The police had no information, so all we can do is start searching the park. Have you got a good powerful torch?'

One was quickly found and Craig fetched another from his car. Mrs Newman had disappeared into the house, and Emma assumed she didn't think it was part of a housekeeper's job to search for a missing person. That left three of them to cover the entire park. Even so, it might not be too difficult to locate him if he was conscious and able to shout.

But what if he had been knocked out—or killed?

To take her mind off such possibilities, she raised a matter which had been puzzling her. 'I don't understand why the horse has only just come back. Mr Stapleton must have had the accident a long time ago.'

'That's easy, miss. He's been having the time of his life eating the grass in the park. He wouldn't be in no hurry to come home.' Mr Newman turned to Craig. 'Do you think we should spread out a bit, sir?'

He agreed and the two men separated, leaving Emma in the middle since she had no torch. It was amazing how the powerful beams lit up the park, disturbing sheep, rabbits and even birds. They walked steadily, shouting every few minutes and pausing to listen. After a while the hitherto level ground dipped sharply and became uneven, and they slowed down on account of various obstructions, such as fallen trees, odd branches and clumps of reeds.

Anne Stapleton would be out of her mind with worry by now, Emma reflected, making a careful descent of what appeared to be a sort of dell. She was glad she was wearing her sturdy hospital shoes, though they couldn't prevent her from becoming wet to the knees. With the lower part of her clothing clinging uncomfortably to her legs, she stumbled and almost fell.

'Are you OK, Emma?' Craig called.

She had saved herself from falling by clutching a

low branch. As she paused, to regain her balance, Craig swung his torch towards her and she gave a sharp exclamation.

'Come over here—quickly!'

'What's the matter? Have you hurt yourself?' He came leaping across the slope towards where she was still embracing the branch.

'Not me.' She pointed at something a few yards further down. 'Look! I don't think we need search any longer.'

Ron Stapleton lay in a strangely crumpled position with one leg at an awkward angle. He looked ghastly in the torchlight, which turned his face into a pattern of planes and hollows. His eyes were closed and his forehead was smeared with blood from a gash still oozing. The hard hat, which had protected him to some extent, had been forced to one side.

Mr Newman came hurrying to join them and gazed in horror at his employer. 'Is he dead, sir? He looks awful to me.'

'Oh, no, he's not dead.' Craig had his fingers on the jugular vein in the neck. 'But he's been lying here for far too long and we must get him to hospital as soon as possible. I don't like the look of that leg and there may be other injuries. Will you please hurry back to the house, Mr Newman, and ring for an ambulance? Tell them it's urgent, because he's certainly suffering from exposure.'

'I can't think why he came into this place,' the man said as he started to scramble up the steep side of the dell. 'The horse doesn't like it and I reckon that's why he threw him. Horses have a lot of sense when it comes to things like that.'

Emma was down on her knees in the long grass, wiping mud and blood from their patient's face with some tissues she had found in her pocket. Craig joined her and began a slow and careful examination.

'I can't be sure without X-rays,' he said when he had finished, 'but I haven't found any other fracture apart from the leg, though he's bound to have severe bruising. You can cover him up now.'

She picked up the rug which Mr Newman had been carrying and tucked it round the injured man as far as possible without trying to alter his position.

'I would have expected him to come round before now,' Craig said thoughtfully. 'He must be very badly concussed and he may have been here for four or five hours. That could be serious in November.'

Emma murmured agreement. She was trying to disguise the fact that she was shivering and she wished she had a rug like the one covering Mr Stapleton. She wrapped her arms round herself and leaned back against a tree-trunk.

'You're cold,' Craig said immediately, 'and I can't say I'm any too warm myself. We must do something about it.' He swung the torchlight round and it illuminated a fallen tree not far away. 'Let's go and sit on that and try and pretend we're not soaking wet from the knees down.'

He took Emma's cold hand in one that wasn't much warmer and they made their way carefully along the slope. 'If we sit very close together,' he went on, 'maybe we'll generate a little warmth.'

Emma thought it more than likely. She was feeling better already, and when they sat down, and he put his arm round her, she felt a delicious sense of contentment spreading over her. And not just contentment either, but something far more exhilarating which was close to happiness.

She couldn't remember having felt like that for a long, long time.

Craig's arm tightened. 'This was a good idea,' he said softly in her ear.

'I'm certainly much warmer,' Emma agreed.

His lips nuzzled her cheek, sending tremors all down her spine. 'Your face is as cold as ice,' he complained, and they both laughed.

But when he started to kiss her in earnest, she panicked. She knew it meant nothing, but she was afraid even of light-hearted dalliance because it might lead to further pain.

'Listen!' She sat up abruptly. 'I'm sure I heard a siren.'

Craig stiffened as he strained his ears. 'Then you were wrong,' he said firmly. 'It couldn't possibly get here as quickly as this.'

But he had taken the hint. Although his arm remained round her shoulders, he no longer hovered on the brink of lovemaking, and instead he began to talk briskly about the practice.

'It was a good thing I asked Sammy Cox to take surgery for me. We're sometimes busier in the evenings than we are in the mornings. Did I tell you we knew each other at medical school?' Not waiting for a reply, he continued on the same subject. 'It's strange we should both turn up here in this neck of the woods.'

To Emma's surprise, he leaned forward and peered into her face. 'Aren't you going to tear me off a strip for daring to call Saxham a neck of the woods?' An odd little smile tilted one corner of his mouth.

Emma returned the smile, glad that she had restrained herself. 'I was only thinking it's an odd description to apply to a seaside place.'

'You're right there!' He paused and then asked with unusual diffidence, 'Do you still feel worked up about the hospital closing?'

'Of course I do!' She was instantly on the defensive. 'I keep thinking about it, and what I can do to start a protest. I was wondering about getting up a petition——'

Craig was not listening to her and Emma knew why. This time there really was an ambulance siren in the distance, and coming rapidly nearer.

'You stay here and I'll go up to the top and wave them in the right direction,' he said.

There followed several minutes of rapid and controlled action. Ron Stapleton was still deeply unconscious and the first priority was to immobolise his leg. The paramedics were cheerful and experienced, and it was quickly done and the rug replaced with a red blanket. Then the stretcher was carried up the slope without fuss, and loaded into the ambulance.

'He's going to be all right, isn't he?' Emma burst out as they watched its departure across the grass.

Craig glanced at her in surprise. 'You a nurse and asking that daft question!' he chided her gently. 'You know I can't possibly give you a definite answer, but I'm about eighty per cent sure he'll be OK. That satisfy you?'

'Yes, of course. I'm sorry I was so silly. It's—it's just that I keep thinking about his wife, waiting all this time and then getting news of this sort.'

They began to walk across the grass and suddenly she tripped over a tussock. Craig immediately put out a hand to steady her, and then linked his arm in hers.

'Can't have you spraining your ankle,' he said softly. 'I don't want to have to carry you back to the car.'

Emma caught her breath and wondered what it would be like to be cradled in his arms. Disturbing, to say the least! But probably he wouldn't carry her that way at all. A fireman's lift would be much easier, though horribly undignified for the person being carried.

And not in the least romantic.

CHAPTER FIVE

IT WAS raining in the morning. As Emma cycled through the puddles under grey skies, and with a cold wet head-wind, she thought how lucky they had all been the previous day. It could have been disastrous for the unconscious man if he had lain there for hours being rained on.

He was very much in her mind when she reached the hospital, and her first question to Maggie Dereham, the night staff nurse, concerned him.

'He came round about midnight,' Maggie told her, 'very confused to find himself in hospital with a leg in plaster and some stitches in his forehead.'

'Who looked after him?' Emma asked in a carefully schooled voice.

'Apparently Dr Norbury arrived soon after the ambulance—I wasn't here then, of course—and when the X-rays showed the leg had a vertical fracture, he said he'd see to it.'

'More like a crack, I suppose,' Emma suggested.

'That's right. Mr Stapleton's OK otherwise, apart from two cracked ribs and lots of bruises. He's to be kept very quiet, though, because of the concussion.'

They had met on the landing and Emma began to take off her wet raincoat. 'Does he remember he's the father of a newborn baby?' she asked casually.

'Oh, yes, he seems quite clear about that, and very annoyed because his wife will have to visit him instead of the other way round. He seems to think he was on his way here when he had the accident, but he's dreadfully muddled about it and has no idea how it happened.'

Emma longed to ask whether the new father's attitude towards his daughter had changed, but Maggie might not know about that so she decided to say nothing. The way to find out was to visit Anne Stapleton at the earliest opportunity.

As always, there was a lot to do at that time of the morning, and Emma was not able to carry out her intention until she took the breakfast tray in. Anne was feeding the baby when she entered and she looked up with a faint smile. She was still very pale, but there was a serenity about her which was new, and rather strange considering what had happened.

'How are you feeling this morning?' Emma asked cautiously, unhooking the chart and studying it.

'Much better than yesterday, thank you. I know it sounds crazy after what happened to Ron, but I really am.'

Emma smiled. 'Does that mean what I think it means?'

'Probably. I expect you're referring to my husband's disappointment because Rosemary—that's what I want to call her—wasn't a boy.' Anne drew a deep breath and her eyes shone. 'He got over that quite quickly and, of course, he was going to tell me as soon as he got here—only he was unconscious and lying on a stretcher.'

Emma sat down on the bed and observed that Rosemary was sucking in a very businesslike way. 'That must have been a most dreadful shock for you.'

'It was at first, but as soon as I learned he wasn't badly hurt I was just so thankful he was safe, and in a way it's nice having him here in the room opposite this one. He's very cross about the accident, though. He prides himself on his horsemanship. Do you think he'll remember how it came about when he's better?'

'It's very probable,' Emma assured her. 'You do realise your husband must be kept very quiet because of the concussion?'

'Oh, yes, I'll be very good.' Anne held her baby up against her shoulder and tried rather amateurishly to produce some burps. Gently, Emma took the infant from her and showed her the most effective way of doing it. As the warm little head, so touchingly incapable of keeping upright, nestled into her shoulder she experienced a wave of emotion. She had always loved babies and somehow this one seemed special, due to all the trauma which had attended her birth.

Reluctantly she handed her back. 'I'll go across and visit your husband now, and then get on with my work. Don't forget to eat your breakfast!'

To Emma's surprise, she found Craig in Ron Stapleton's room with the chart in his hand. The patient appeared to be asleep.

'You've started work early!' she exclaimed.

'All due to the weather. It's such a foul morning that I'm afraid Rex only got a very short walk on the heath. It's nearer than the beach.' He moved closer and held out the chart. 'Looks quite satisfactory, all things considered.'

Emma glanced at the figures, painstakingly entered by Maggie throughout the night. If everything continued going well it looked as though he would be going home as soon as the concussion was better.

'Have you seen his wife this morning?' Craig asked.

'I've just come from her room. It looks as though she's taken the accident extraordinarily well. In fact, she's a lot happier than she was yesterday at this time.' Lowering her voice, in case the patient was only dozing and might suddenly wake up, she explained about his change of heart with regard to the baby's sex. 'Are you going to see her?'

'I hadn't intended doing so—strictly speaking, she's Sammy's patient, not mine.' He clipped the chart back into place, gave Emma a friendly smile and departed.

She stood quite still for a moment, her thoughts chaotic behind her calm exterior. What was happening to her? Why should she have reacted so alarmingly to Craig's presence? She had, she knew, hidden it well, but there was no denying that just standing close to him had turned her emotions upside down.

It had got to stop!

With a sigh, she was about to turn away when she noticed that Ron's eyes were open. 'Hello!'

Smiling, she went up to the bed. 'How are you this morning?'

'Bloody sore! I reckon I've bruised every bone in my body.' He frowned and winced at the same time. 'I still can't imagine what made Cavalier throw me like that—not that I actually remember anything about it, but I was told I'd been thrown.'

'I expect it'll all come back to you before long,' Emma soothed. 'In the meantime, don't try to force your brain to recall what happened. You'll recover much more quickly if you just let it stay idle.'

'Easier said than done,' he grumbled.

'Meanwhile I'll make your bed more comfortable.' She raised his head carefully and turned the pillows. He had blond hair like his wife's, only darker, and a small moustache with a gingerish gleam. His eyes were blue-grey with dark shadows round them, and one was developing a magnificent black eye.

'Have you seen your wife this morning?' she went on, straightening the bedclothes.

'I think so.' He managed a smile. 'I believe she looked in earlier. I expect she'll come along later on and bring the baby with her.'

'You've got a lovely child,' Emma said carefully. 'Strong and healthy.'

An odd look passed over his face. 'Thanks to my accident, I haven't seen much of her. I was a bit disappointed at first that she wasn't a boy—it matters when you belong to an old family like ours—but I soon got over that. We've got plenty of time to try again.' He half closed his eyes and suddenly looked desperately tired.

Emma was conscience-stricken. All her nursing instincts were telling her she was letting him talk far too much.

'If Matron catches me in here, nattering away to you, she'll have me shot at dawn. Have another sleep now, and then you'll be ready for your wife's visit.'

As she closed the door behind her she felt well-satisfied with the conversation, even if she hadn't entirely followed the rules. It was good news that Ron had changed his attitude towards his daughter without any outside pressure being put on him, and it augured well for the family's future.

It was the custom at the cottage hospital for Miss Lenton and her senior nurses to drink their mid-morning coffee together in her private office on the ground floor. That morning the other staff nurse was a woman named Judy Garner, who had unnaturally black hair and a ruddy complexion. She was divorced and had a teenage family.

They were an ill-assorted trio, with Emma so much the youngest. Sometimes Judy dominated the conversation, holding forth about her family and their numerous problems, but today it was Miss Lenton who had a lot to say.

'I drove over to Stonebridge yesterday evening and had supper with the matron—you remember she's a friend of mine? We talked quite a lot about the proposed new hospital. She's absolutely delighted that hers is to be replaced with a fine modern building.'

'You can understand that,' Judy said. 'It used to be a workhouse.'

'I agree.' The matron took a sip of coffee. 'But that doesn't mean we have to be pleased too—about our own, I mean. Saxham has been well looked after and is nowhere near ready for demolition.'

Demolition—what a dreadful word to be applied to this dear, familiar building, so much loved locally. Emma almost choked over her coffee.

'Did she say whether the site has been chosen?' she asked.

'There's a meeting some time to select the most suitable one out of three. I don't know where they are.'

'One thing's for sure,' Judy said gloomily, 'none of them will be as handy for Saxham people as this one. I don't know if I shall be able to keep on nursing if the new hospital is, say, more than five miles away. I can't afford to run a car.'

Miss Lenton poured second cups of coffee for them. 'One feels so helpless in the grip of authority. I wish there was something we could do.' She glanced across at her younger staff nurse. 'Emma, my dear, haven't you any ideas?'

'I've been thinking about it ever since we heard the news.' She hesitated, and then drew a deep breath and plunged in. 'I'm wondering if we could get up a petition. It's done a lot nowadays, though mostly on a bigger scale than we could manage——'

Judy interrupted. 'People collect hundreds of signatures and take them up to Downing Street. I've seen it on TV lots of times.'

'Downing Street wouldn't be interested in our

little problems,' Miss Lenton put in.

'I realise that, of course, but we could still collect signatures and send them to the local authority. I'm sure nearly everybody in Saxham would be glad to sign.'

'How many people would you need to help you organise a thing like that?' Judy asked. 'It's no good counting on me because I just wouldn't have the time. You can't imagine the amount of work my three make.'

'I don't know how many people I'd need until I get started.'

Miss Lenton was looking at her watch and Emma suddenly realised they had overrun their coffee-break by ten minutes. She hastily drained her cup and stood up. As she was on her way back to the wards it occurred to her that the other two had, without a word being spoken, taken it for granted that she would take charge of the petition.

It was a challenge and she rose to it eagerly. After all, for family reasons, she probably felt more strongly about the closure of Saxham hospital than anyone else.

They were busy that day, with several patients going home and others arriving in their place. One of these, to Emma's astonishment, was her own great-aunt Mary from Cliff House who, at ninety-two, was the eldest. Gina Baines, the schoolgirl with abdominal pains, was the youngest.

'Those tiresome pains have started up again,' her mother told Emma. 'Dr Roberts says there's no point in messing about any longer. He's now pretty sure she has a grumbling appendix and he's arranging for somebody to come and do the operation tomorrow.'

Emma shook down a thermometer and put it into Gina's mouth. The girl was obviously in some discomfort and her bright cheeks suggested fever.

'I hoped Dr Roberts would do the job himself,' Mrs Baines confided, 'but he pointed out he was a physician, not a surgeon. It seems strange to me to have a hospital, even one this size, without a resident surgeon.'

'This is a GPs' hospital,' Emma explained, knowing that the Baines family had only recently moved to Saxham. 'That means only very minor operations can be performed by the local doctors.'

When she had seen Gina settled as comfortably as possible, she went to visit her aged relative.

'What are you doing here, Aunt Mary?' She sat down beside the bed and laid her fingers on the bony wrist.

'It's not my choice, I assure you.' The gruff old voice matched the wrinkled face and knob of scanty white hair, but the vigorous tone in which the words were spoken could have belonged to a much younger person. 'Dr Roberts called this morning and told me I was looking peaky. Such nonsense! I always look the same at my age, and that's not exactly blooming. What else does he expect, I'd like to know? He would have it that I needed a bit of looking after and so here I am.' She looked round disparagingly. 'I haven't been in hospital since I broke my leg when I was sixty.'

'You seemed all right to me when I called the

other day, but I expect the doctor knows what he's doing.'

Miss Mayfield snorted rudely. 'That's open to doubt! I look after myself very nicely at Cliff House. I've got my bed downstairs and everything handy, and I make sure I have one good meal a day. If I choose to live on bread and butter and cups of tea at other times, that's my own affair.'

Emma didn't argue. She knew it was useless. But when Dr Roberts looked in later on, and described Miss Mayfield as his favourite patient, she seized the opportunity to asked why he had had her hospitalised.

'Her heart's a bit dicky.' He smoothed his neat little beard. 'Nothing very serious, but I thought a little cosseting might do her good. One of the good things about this hospital is that you can admit patients for that sort of purpose, which you certainly couldn't do in an ordinary hospital.'

Emma seized on the comment eagerly. 'Then *you* don't want it to be pulled down and replaced by a big impersonal place miles away?'

'I most certainly don't.' He hesitated. 'But I'm afraid it may come to that. Saxham isn't at all the sort of hospital to appeal to the powers-that-be.'

She wanted to tell him that she was going to fight the closure as hard as she could, but he was obviously in a hurry and so she refrained. She was longing to discuss it with someone, though, and that evening she told her mother about it.

At first Ruth was enthusiastic, and then she began to have doubts.

'It's a big job, Emma, and you really need a proper committee to draw up plans——'

'A committee! Whatever would I want that for? Committees always argue and waste a lot of time. All I need is some people to help me with collecting signatures.'

'Well, you can count me in for that. It might be a good idea to have a table at the Saturday market and ask people to sign there and then——'

'That's a super idea! Do you think you could prepare the sheets of paper for me—get them ruled up and ready for signatures?'

Ruth willingly agreed, and Emma sat down to make a list of possible helpers. It was not an easy task. The cottage hospital had a lot of part-time nurses, all of whom had homes and families to look after in addition to their work. Judy Garner had already stated frankly that she would be unable to help. The younger nurses might be willing, though, and probably would be better at the job.

Before she went to bed Emma had produced a list of possibilities, and during the next few days she seized every opportunity to put forward her plan to the various people concerned. Some were keen to help, others protested that their boyfriends took up all their time when they weren't on duty, and a few obviously couldn't care less about the fate of Saxham hospital. But by the weekend Emma had enough names to make the scheme worthwhile. She managed to draw up a rota of nurses to look after the table at the Saturday market, but found it impossible to lend a hand herself. Her own day off was Sunday, which was not a very good day for canvassing.

Off and on, during the Saturday, she wondered

how the girls were getting on.

They were busy at the hospital. A triple car crash on the outskirts of the town had brought them a crop of new patients, mostly teenagers with minor injuries. They were not bad enough to be glad to rest and their taste in television programmes did not please the older patients. Miss Mayfield, in particular, complained bitterly about it.

Gina Baines thought it was great. She was making a good recovery from her appendicectomy but not very anxious to go home.

'I'm glad we were wrong about her pains being psychosomatic,' Dr Roberts said privately to Emma. 'I don't like to think a young girl is so unhappy at home she gives herself the symptoms of appendicitis. It's very difficult to cope with that sort of thing. The pain is real yet it has no physical cause. Has she said anything about the situation to you?'

'Not much, but her mother's new partner never comes to see her. I suppose he knows he wouldn't be welcome.' Emma hesitated. 'You mentioned counselling when she was here before. Have you thought any more about it?'

'I abandoned the idea when her abdominal trouble turned out to be real, but I shall have to go into it now, I'm afraid.'

They had been talking on the landing—the usual place for conversations concerning patients—and Emma was standing with her back to the stairs. As she said goodbye to Dr Roberts she half turned round, and saw Craig coming up from the hall.

'Hi!' He greeted her cheerfully. 'It's a couple of days since I saw my patient so I thought I'd better check up on him.'

His sudden appearance had given her an odd sort of feeling and she had to work hard at hiding it.

'Mr Stapleton? He's doing fine, but his memory is still a little muddled.'

'Is he fit to go home, do you think?'

'That's for you to say—you're the doctor!' She laughed up into his face, suddenly feeling light-hearted.

'I'll make up my mind when I've seen him. Are you going to escort me in the good old-fashioned way which seems to suit this place?'

Emma's face changed. 'You never let slip an opportunity to poke fun at our hospital, do you?'

To her mortification, Craig burst out laughing. 'You're so vulnerable that I can't resist the chance to tease you. You should try and grow a thicker skin.'

'But I don't want to—I feel passionate about what you call "this place". I want it to go on forever, and——' she tilted her chin and looked him straight in the eye '—for your information, the petition to save it is getting off the ground today at the Saturday market.'

'How come you're not there?'

'I've got to work, haven't I? We're too busy for me to have a day off. And that reminds me— you've come here to see a patient, not to jeer at the hospital which is looking after him.'

'I'm not jeering at it—I wouldn't dream of it.' He was suddenly as angry as Emma had been a moment before. 'I'm sorry you can't take a perfectly innocent bit of ragging without getting steamed up.'

Horrified at what was happening, Emma glanced round, and was relieved to see that there were no witnesses to a row between doctor and nurse at Saxham cottage hospital. She was quite sure nothing like that had ever happened before—at least not in her time.

Without another word, she led the way to Ron Stapleton's private room.

He was sitting up in bed, looking a great deal better apart from the wonderful colours of his bruises. He greeted them cheerfully.

'I think I've just remembered why I went down into the dell! I thought I could see a fox's earth—a new one—but I wasn't sure whether it was just that the rabbits had been extra busy. There's a lot of undergrowth there, you know, and it's hard to get a good view from the top.'

'Did you ever find out?' Craig asked.

'I don't think so. Cavalier hates that place and he took me under a low branch to pay me out, with the result that I came off. I'd probably have been OK on level ground but I fell awkwardly. The rest you know.'

'You were lucky on the whole. Your amnesia hasn't lasted very long, and that type of fracture—though it takes nearly as long to heal—isn't likely to give any trouble. When would you like to go home?'

'We thought perhaps on Monday,' Ron said diffidently. 'That will give the Newmans time to get a bed downstairs for me and make a temporary bedroom in the library. There's a toilet quite close, with a shower. Does that sound like a good idea to you?'

'Very good indeed, provided your wife is agreeable.'

'We had breakfast together and discussed it then, and she says she's longing to get home and start looking after Rosemary all by herself. It's been great having her here while I was still so muddled, but that's over now that the last piece has fallen into place.'

'It was lucky that we didn't need her room,' Emma put in from the corner, where she had been standing quietly.

Ron seemed to become aware of her presence. 'I don't think I've ever thanked you for the part you played in my rescue. I didn't know about it at first, of course.' His gaze switched to Craig. 'If the two of you hadn't organised a search, I probably wouldn't be here now.'

There was a slightly emotional pause, and then Craig made a move towards the door.

'I probably shan't see you here again. Miss Lenton will check that you're fit to leave on Monday, and unless your chart suddenly goes mad I can't see anything likely to prevent it. My very best wishes for your complete recovery.' With sudden formality, he returned to the bed and shook hands.

'Nice bloke,' he commented to Emma outside in the corridor.

'Yes.' She halted. 'I'll go and see his wife, and tell her the good news.'

'Hang on a minute.' He put out his hand and

caught her by the arm. 'Rex is wondering when you're coming for another walk with us on the beach. Have you got a day off soon?'

'Tomorrow,' Emma said, not giving herself time to think.

'Won't you be busy with your petition?'

'I didn't think Sunday would be a good day. People go to church, or out for drives—all that sort of thing. I've got some time off on Monday afternoon and I thought I might make a start then.'

'So you could come walking, weather permitting?'

Afraid he might read in her eyes how much she wanted to say yes, Emma veiled them with her lashes. 'I'll come,' she said slowly, 'if we make a rule that we won't talk about the petition.'

'That's certainly OK by me. See you at the end of the promenade about ten o'clock.'

That evening Emma made a point of listening to the weather forecast, and was quite ridiculously pleased to learn that Sunday was likely to be fine and probably sunny. She went to bed in a happy frame of mind and, for once, not bothering to analyse her reasons for feeling that way.

Craig was waiting, with an impatient Rex, just where the cliffs began. The weatherman had been accurate in his forecast and the beautiful morning reminded Emma of that Saturday a couple of weeks ago when Pete and Kevin had attempted to dig out a cave. She hadn't seen them since and she hoped they had learnt their lesson.

Man and dog greeted her with every appearance

of pleasure, and they set off along the sandy shingle at a good pace.

'Do you fancy a swim?' Emma asked.

'No, I don't. I shan't venture into the North Sea again until June. How about you?'

'It's usually July for me, but that's very cowardly.' Emma hesitated. 'I don't seem to go in the sea very much at all nowadays.'

'Why not?'

The question floored her, though she knew the answer. It was because Paul was no longer here. He had been the one who was really keen on swimming, and after the bank he worked for had transferred him to a London branch she hadn't had the heart to swim alone. Not even before she realised that he had seized the opportunity to sever all contact with her.

'I'm still waiting for an answer,' Craig reminded her gently.

Emma made an effort to dredge up something acceptable. 'People don't always have reasons for the things they do—or don't do.'

'True, but I suspect that you have. Did you perhaps have a frightening experience in the sea and nearly get drowned?'

'Oh, no—it was nothing like that.'

As soon as the words had escaped, she bit her lip. She was not at all surprised when Craig pounced.

'So there *was* a reason! Are you going to let me into the secret or must it remain locked in your heart forever?'

Emma was beginning to get rattled. 'I never knew such a man for probing into things people don't want to talk about. I didn't come on this walk to be put through an inquisition.'

Greatly to her surprise, he was instantly contrite. 'I'm sorry. I thought we were having a light-hearted conversation—a sort of verbal sparring of no importance. I didn't realise we were talking about something that mattered to you.'

Emma was silent, but she was thinking furiously. A seagull, one of a crowd which had been circling overhead, swooped down to investigate a piece of seaweed and was chased by Rex. The soft plash of the waves suddenly grew louder as the wash of a ship reached the shore. A fisherman sat motionless on the beach, protected from the light wind by his huge umbrella.

She noticed none of these things. Her mind was back in the past, back in that summer when Paul had disappeared. And suddenly she knew she wanted to tell Craig about him.

'If you really want to know,' she began, in a casual offhand sort of way, 'I used to swim a lot with my boyfriend, and then his job took him to London and—and—I never saw him or heard from him again.' Suddenly she was struggling with a lump in her throat.

It was absurd to feel emotional about it after all this time. It must be because she had never talked about Paul's disappearance to anyone except, in the beginning, her mother. It certainly wasn't because she still loved him. He had hurt her badly, and humiliated her too, but the pain had gone now.

Or so she had believed. And yet sometimes, in her weaker moments, she wondered how she

OFFICIAL RULES
NO PURCHASE NECESSARY TO ENTER
MILLION DOLLAR SWEEPSTAKES (III)

To enter, follow the directions published. Method of entry may vary. For eligibility, entries must be received no later than March 31, 1996. No liability is assumed for printing errors, lost, late or misdirected entries.

To determine winners, the sweepstakes numbers on submitted entries will be compared against a list of randomly, pre-selected prizewinning numbers. In the event all prizes are not claimed via the return of prizewinning numbers, random drawings will be held from among all other entries received to award unclaimed prizes.

Prizewinners will be determined no later than June 30, 1996. Selection of winning numbers and random drawings are under the supervision of D. L. Blair, Inc., an independent judging organisation whose decisions are final. Limit: one prize to a family or organisation. No substitution will be made for any prize, except as offered. Taxes and duties on all prizes are the sole responsibility of winners. Winners will be notified by mail. Odds of winning are determined by the number of eligible entries distributed and received.

Sweepstakes open to residents of the U.S. (except Puerto Rico), Canada, Europe and Taiwan who are 18 years of age or older, except employees and immediate family members of Torstar Corp., D.L. Blair, Inc., their affiliates, subsidiaries, and all other agencies, entities and persons connected with the use, marketing or conduct of this sweepstakes. All applicable laws and regulations apply. Sweepstakes offer void wherever prohibited by law. Any litigation within the province of Quebec respecting the conduct and awarding of a prize in this sweepstakes must be submitted to the Regies des Loteries et Courses du Quebec. In order to win a prize, residents of Canada will be required to answer a time-limited arithmetical skill-testing question to be administered by mail.

Winners of major prizes (Grand through Fourth) will be obligated to sign and return an affidavit of Eligibility and Release of Liability within 30 days of notification. In the event of non-compliance within this time period or if a prize is returned as undeliverable, D. L. Blair, Inc. may at its sole discretion, award that prize to an alternate winner. By acceptance of their prize, winners consent to use of their names, photographs or other likeness for purposes of advertising, trade and promotion on behalf of Torstar Corp., its affiliates and subsidiaries, without further compensation unless prohibited by law. Torstar Corp. and D.L. Blair, Inc., their affiliates and subsidiaries not responsible for errors in printing of sweepstakes and prize winning numbers. In the event a duplication of a prize winning number occurs, a random drawing will be held from among all entries received with that prize winning number to award that prize.

This sweepstakes is presented by Torstar Corp., their subsidiaries, and affiliates in conjunction with book, merchandise and/or product offerings. *The number of prizes to be awarded and their value are as follows: Grand Prize - $1,000,000 (payable at $33,333.33 a year for 30 years): First Prize - $50,000; Second Prize - $10,000; Third Prize - $5,000; Fourth Prizes - $1,000 each; 10 Fifth Prizes - $250 each; 1000 Sixth Prizes - $100 each. Values of all prizes are in U.S. currency. Prizes in each level will be presented in different creative executions, including various currencies, vehicles, merchandise and travel. Any presentation of a prize level in a currency other than U.S. currency represents an approximate equivalent to the U.S. currency prize for that level, at that time. Prize winners will have the opportunity of selecting a prize offered for that level; however, the actual non U.S. currency equivalent prize, if offered and selected, shall be awarded at the exchange rate existing 3:00 P.M. New York time on March 31, 1996. A travel prize option, if offered and selected by the winner, must be completed within 12 months of selection and is subject to: travelling companion (s) completing and returning of a Release of Liability prior to travel; and hotel and flight accommodations availability. For current list of all prize options offered within prize levels, send a self-addressed, stamped envelope to MILLION DOLLAR SWEEPSTAKES (III) Prize Options, Harlequin Mills & Boon, UK: PO Box 236, Croydon, Surrey, CR9 3RU, IRELAND: PO Box 4546, Dublin 24. For a list of prize winners (available after July 31, 1996) send a separate, stamped self-addressed envelope to: Million Dollar Sweepstakes (III) Winners, Harlequin Mills & Boon, UK: PO Box 236, Croydon, Surrey, CR9 3RU. IRELAND PO Box 4546, Dublin 24.

*U.K. equivalent prize values at the time of printing. Grand Prize - £600,000; First Prize - £30,000; Second Prize - £6,000; Third Prize - £3,000; 3 Fourth Prizes - £600 each; 10 Fifth Prizes - £150 each; 1,000 Sixth Prizes - £60 each.

ALTERNATE MEANS OF ENTRY
NO PURCHASE NECESSARY

To enter the Prize Draw without requesting books and gifts, tick box on coupon. Or you may hand print "£600,000 Lotto" plus your name and address on a postcard and send it to:- £600,000 Lotto, Harlequin Mills & Boon, P.O. Box 70, Croydon, Surrey CR93JE, and we'll assign a Prize Draw number to you.

You are invited to play
£600,000 LOTTO!

LOTTO CARD No: FA178139

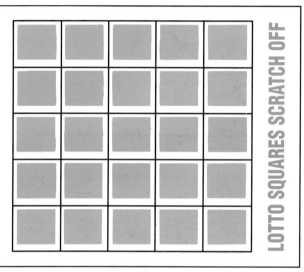

LOTTO SQUARES SCRATCH OFF

Instructions: Using a coin, scratch away silver squares, in a straight line (across, down or diagonal) until 5 hearts are revealed. Doing this makes you eligible for a chance to win one of the following prizes: Grand Prize, £600,000; First prize £30,000; Second Prize £6,000; Third Prize £3,000; Fourth Prize £600. VOID IF MORE THAN 5 SILVER SQUARES ARE SCRATCHED AWAY.

AND... YOU CAN CLAIM UP TO 4 FREE BOOKS, AN AUSTRIAN CRYSTAL NECKLACE AND A MYSTERY GIFT ABSOLUTELY FREE.

To register your entry in the £600,000 Prize Draw and to claim your free books and gifts simply return this card. See the coupon overleaf.

Accepting free books places you under no obligation to buy anything. You may keep the books and gifts and return the shipping label marked 'cancel'. Otherwise, every month we'll send you four brand new Love on Call novels to read and enjoy for just £1.99* each - the same price as the books in the shops. There is no extra charge for postage and packing and no hidden extras.

We hope that you'll want to remain a subscriber. But the choice is yours - continue or cancel, anytime at all. So why not take up our invitation, with no risk of any kind. You'll be glad you did!

*Prices subject to change without notice.

DON'T HESITATE REPLY TODAY!

FREE BOOKS CERTIFICATE

YES! Please send me the free books and gifts to which I am entitled and no obligation, as explained overleaf, and that I may cancel at anytime simply by writing to you.

If you would like to enter the £600,000 prize draw but would prefer not to receive books please tick box. ☐

Ms / Mrs / Miss / Mr _____

Address _____

_____

_____

_____ Postcode _____

8A5D

HARLEQUIN MILLS & BOON
FREEPOST
P.O. BOX 70
CROYDON
SURREY
CR9 9EL

NO
STAMP
NEEDED

would feel if he returned suddenly and asked for her forgiveness.

Craig's fingers, warm and comforting, curled round her hand and they walked on for a moment in silence.

Then he said, 'How long ago did all this happen?'

'Two years last summer.' Recovering her composure, and determined to make a good job of it, she went on to tell him that it had been at about the same time as her father was killed.

'That really was tough!'

Emma managed a rather shaky laugh. 'That's what I felt at the time, and still do, as a matter of fact, though I honestly do try hard not to let myself think about it.'

'I felt there was something—different about you, but I never imagined there was such a grim story hidden in your past.' He gave her hand a squeeze and retained hold of it.

They passed the steps and continued along the beach. It stretched ahead of them, deserted and treacherous, with its crumbling cliffs a constant reminder of danger.

For once Emma was oblivious of the seashore she loved so much, nor was she thinking about her recent baring of the secret recesses of her heart. After a few moments of indecision, she put her thoughts into words.

'Now that I've satisfied your curiosity about me, how about a bit of reciprocation? Just now and then I feel a little curious about you.' Smiling, she looked up into his face. 'Do you feel in the mood to come clean?'

She thought he seemed startled, and yet it was only fair that he should have to put up with the sort of probing he had subjected her to. At his age he must have been in love a few times, even if he wasn't just now, and there was no proof of that. He might have a girlfriend in Eastbourne.

'You want to know about my women?' he said slowly.

'That's the idea,' Emma agreed cheerfully.

Craig glanced round. At a little distance there was the whitened trunk of a tree, long ago fallen from somewhere on the cliff-top.

'Let's sit down for a few minutes. The romantic tale I have to tell requires your full attention.'

Intrigued, Emma allowed herself to be towed up a shingle bank. As she perched precariously on the trunk she was conscious of a change of mood. A moment ago she had been feeling quite light-hearted—now she was actually *afraid* of what she might be going to hear.

CHAPTER SIX

IT SEEMED to Emma a long time before Craig began to speak, but she tried to wait patiently. She sensed that he had withdrawn from her to a great distance, but at last he sighed, shifted his position on the uncomfortable seat, and made a brief statement.

'I used to be married, then I was divorced, and now I suppose you could call me a widower.' His smile was strained and held no amusement. 'And that, my dear Emma, is the story of my love-life in the proverbial nutshell.'

She gasped, and felt as though she had been hit with a hammer. 'Are you prepared to embroider that a little?' she asked when she had recovered slightly.

'Helen and I met at medical school and fell in love. After a short spell of sharing a flatlet, we decided to risk getting married. To be fair, she was more aware of the dangers than I was.' He paused. 'Sammy Cox was around at the time, and a friend of both of us. Being an onlooker, she could probably tell you more about what went wrong than I could.'

'How long did the marriage last?'

'Two years. It was OK until we got house physician jobs at the same hospital. You presumably trained at a large hospital—you know what the pressure is like for junior doctors.'

Emma remembered very well. Lots of marriages foundered on that rock. 'So what happened then?'

'The stress mounted until it was worse at home than at work, and I suppose the end was inevitable. We had to separate or go under, and the next step, of course, was divorce.'

Emma waited a moment and then said gently, 'You said you were now a widower——?'

'Yes. Horrible word, isn't it? Even worse than widow. After a year or two Helen married again—a consultant this time. I believe they were very happy, but—sadly—she contracted hepatitis B and didn't survive.'

Emma blinked back tears. Impulsively, she slipped her arm into Craig's and pressed close. 'I'm so sorry I caused you to recall all that. It must have been very painful for you.'

'It was certainly painful at the time,' he admitted, 'but there's no need for you to be sorry. I can talk about it now and, in a way, I was glad to do so. It made me realise how far into the past that whole unhappy story has slipped. You mustn't imagine I'm going about carrying a load of misery.' He smiled into her eyes. 'Far from it. I've long ago learnt to regard it as a useful lesson. The only thing which I shall always regret is Helen's death.'

She murmured something, and suddenly became conscious of racing pulses. There was tension of a different sort in the air now, and Craig turned towards her, drawing her even closer with his free arm. He kissed her on the lips, at first gently and then very firmly indeed. And Emma, her eyes closed, felt herself drifting on a sweet, fragile cloud of happiness.

The barking of the dog brought them back to reality. He was at one of his favourite occupations—chasing a seagull—and when it had flown away he came racing up to see why they weren't getting on with the walk.

For a short time Craig resisted Rex's appeal, and then he sighed and released Emma reluctantly. 'You have absolutely no tact,' he admonished the animal.

She laughed, grateful that the dog had turned something which had been threatening to get out of hand into the light-hearted affair it really was. She had enjoyed being kissed by Craig, but she had begun to feel far too emotionally involved for her own peace of mind.

They walked on hand in hand until the marina at the mouth of the River Wick came into sight, and then turned back. When they reached the steps they climbed up them by mutual unspoken consent

'Do you mind if we stop for a moment at Cliff House?' Emma asked. 'I'd like to check everything's OK now that Aunt Mary is in hospital.'

'Is it serious?' Craig looked with interest at the grim building they were approaching.

'Oh, no—she's not ill. Dr Roberts thought a few days of being looked after would do her good. Needless to say, she doesn't agree.'

'I suppose you want to make sure another piece of her back garden hasn't slipped over the cliff?'

'I don't think it's very likely at present—the

weather hasn't been right for cliff-falls.' Emma
led the way up the weedy path. 'Why I wanted
to call in was so I could peep in her kitchen cupboards and make sure she's got a good stock of
sensible tinned food. I daren't even mention such
a thing when she's here.' She took a key out of
her pocket and unlocked the front door. 'Mum
and I have been trying for years to get her to
have Meals on Wheels, but she won't.'

'While you're inside,' Craig said, 'Rex and I
will walk round the house and inspect the situation
in the garden. I don't suppose you'll be long.'

'Do be careful!' Emma exclaimed. 'It really is
very dangerous.'

He grinned and assured her that they would
both be wary of sinister-looking cracks. Not
altogether trusting him, she stepped into a small,
square hall and closed the door behind her.

Immediately a high-pitched old voice called out
from the kitchen, 'Who's that?'

'Aunt Mary!' Emma hurried down the hall and
confronted her aged relative. 'What on earth are
you doing here?'

The old lady was sitting in her favourite chair
near to a large electric fire which was giving out a
good heat. She looked at Emma with an indignant
expression on her face.

'I've got a right to be in my own house,
haven't I?'

'Not when you're supposed to be in hospital.'

'I didn't like it there, so I ordered a taxi and
came home. Any objections?'

Emma could think of plenty, but wisely didn't
mention them. 'I hope you realise you've been

very naughty,' she said instead. 'Dr Roberts won't approve.'

'Dr Roberts can think what he likes,' Miss Mayfield snorted.

There seemed no point in staying any longer. Having ascertained that her great-aunt needed no shopping done for her, Emma said goodbye and went to rejoin Craig, who was waiting by the gate.

'You've been quick,' he commented.

She smiled wryly. 'There was nothing to do. She decided she'd had enough of hospital so she discharged herself and came home by taxi. I found her sitting comfortably in the kitchen and very much in charge of the situation.'

Craig laughed outright. 'Good for her!'

'It's not good at all. Dr Roberts says her heart's a bit rocky and she shouldn't be living alone, but I don't know of any way of stopping her.' She shrugged and changed the subject. 'How did your inspection of the back garden go?'

'I don't think there's any immediate danger, but I wouldn't like my garden to be in that perilous state. Why doesn't the council rehouse her?'

'Because she doesn't want to be rehoused.'

He laughed again and recaptured her hand, but as they walked on towards the High Street, where they would separate, Emma was aware that the happiness she had experienced earlier had evaporated like mist in the sunshine. It was only what she had expected, but she hadn't realised she would mind so much.

The following day the Stapleton family left the hospital, Ron on crutches and Anne proudly carrying the baby. The entire staff on duty at the time assembled in the hall to see them off. Emma brought them down in the lift, and their own car with Mr Newman at the wheel awaited them outside.

'You must come and see us when we get settled in at home,' Anne said, pausing at the bottom of the steps. 'I'll ring you up as soon as I feel like having guests.'

'You mustn't regard me as a guest,' Emma protested, 'but I'd certainly love to pop in to see you and Rosemary.'

'But I want to regard you as a guest—and Dr Norbury too. I shall invite you both to dinner.' The radiant expression Anne had been displaying up to then suddenly faded. 'After all, you and the doctor almost certainly saved Ron's life. He might have died of exposure if you hadn't searched for him.'

Emma shook her head. 'The police would have found him if we hadn't.'

But Anne would have none of it. 'It might have been too late then——' her voice shook '—and I shall always remember that it was you two who insisted on looking for him immediately.'

Emma abandoned the argument as she recalled how worried Mr Newman had been about neglecting the horse. 'Anyway,' she said, smiling, 'I shall look forward to coming over to Pember Hall when you feel fit enough for visitors.'

When they had driven away, she went thoughtfully back upstairs. There was no denying that surprise hadn't been the only emotion she had experienced when the invitation had been issued and she realised it included Craig. It seemed an age since she had gone out with a man on a social occasion.

He came up to the hospital a little later to visit a patient who had been admitted for observation. Miss Fielding was a school-teacher in her forties who was both shy and nervous and looked much older. She had straight brown hair, cut very short and already showing signs of grey, and her skin had a yellowish tinge.

Craig was punctilious in asking Emma to chaperon him while he made his examination. She drew the pretty floral curtains and shut the three of them into a small private world. Talking cheerfully about nothing very much, she folded the bedclothes back not an inch more than necessary, and gently pulled up Miss Fielding's sensible nightdress.

Smiling ruefully at his patient, Craig apologised for cold hands. She smiled valiantly back at him as he began to palpate her abdomen. Emma, watching intently, was looking for signs of flinching but at first she saw none.

'This looks like an old appendicitis scar,' Craig commented. 'Did you have any trouble with adhesions?'

'None at all, Doctor. I got over the operation very quickly and I've been perfectly fit ever since—until recently.'

His careful fingers moved higher up and Emma immediately noticed that Miss Fielding's tension had increased. It almost seemed as though she was bracing herself, but Craig's expression gave nothing away. When he had finished the examination he pulled up the sheet and sat down casually on the edge of the bed.

'Did you—did you find anything?' Miss Fielding asked faintly.

'Nothing specific.' He kept his tone light. 'All the same, this discomfort you've been having needs investigating. I'm arranging for you to have an X-ray tomorrow and then we'll have another talk. In the meantime, I'm putting you on a strict diet—just in case there's any liver trouble.'

Her muddy brown eyes widened but all she said was, 'I shan't mind that. I've had very little appetite lately.

Craig patted her hand in an avuncular way and she blushed. 'Try not to worry. Just look upon this spell in hospital as a holiday and an opportunity for a good rest. Do you like reading?'

'Oh, yes, Doctor——'

'Nurse will take you to the library later on.' He smiled and stood up. 'Goodbye for now.'

Emma walked with him as far as the landing. 'Have you been able to make a diagnosis?' she ventured to ask.

'It's either her liver or gall bladder. Both would account for that yellowish look.' He sighed. 'It could be serious, Emma, but I hope she doesn't realise that.'

Did he know about Anne Stapleton wanting to invite them both to dinner? she wondered as she watched him running downstairs. Probably not, and in any case it might never happen.

That afternoon she made her first contribution to the collecting of signatures for the petition. The market stall on Saturday had been a success, and now it was her turn to do what she could. She had only two hours to spend on it and she chose to call on the big houses near the hospital, one of which was her own old home.

Being in uniform gave her a certain amount of confidence, but the first house was an ordeal, as the occupant turned out to be a very deaf old man who could make no sense at all out of what she was trying to say. Even so, he agreed to sign his name. After that it was easy, and Emma went back on duty feeling she had made a good start.

In order to discourage Miss Fielding from brooding too much, she gave her a full account of her afternoon.

'I'd heard they were talking of closing our hospital,' Miss Fielding said sadly. 'It certainly does seem a shame. There are a lot of people in Saxham who have cause to be grateful to it.'

It was just what Emma wanted to hear. 'With so many people feeling strongly about the threatened closure, surely the authorities ought to listen to what they've got to say?'

'One would think so, and it's wonderful what can be accomplished by enthusiasm,' Miss Fielding said thoughtfully. 'I wish you the best of luck in your campaign. When I'm better, if there's anything I can do you have only to ask.'

Emma was touched by the offer.

'That's very kind of you, and I won't forget.'

It would have been nice if Craig had been equally sympathetic.

He kept his promise about returning to see his patient the following day after she had had her X-rays, but before visiting her he went to the office with Emma to study them.

They loked at them in silence, their expressions intent.

'Not as bad as I feared,' Craig said eventually, 'but she'll have to see a consultant at Heathbury, and probably he'll want a proper scan. I'll get on to it as soon as I've seen her.'

'Do you think he'll operate?'

'It's probable. The gallstones are too big to be dispersed, but that's up to him.'

They went into the ward and approached Miss Fielding's bed. This time there was no need to draw the curtains. She listened without interruption to what Craig had to say and then burst into what—for her—was a strong protest.

'Do I have to go to Heathbury, Doctor? I don't mind being in this dear little hospital, where everybody's so friendly, but I dread going to a big place where I don't know anybody, and nobody knows me either—or cares,' she added bitterly.

He reproved her gently. 'You mustn't say things like that. People will care about you just as much at Heathbury as they do here, and they've got all sorts of marvellous equipment for diagnosis— even a wonderful scanner called an MRI——'

'I don't know what that is and I don't want to know! You found out from ordinary X-rays that I'd got gallstones, so why do I have to have anything else?'

With the utmost patience, Craig did his best to explain that the new scanner would show a more detailed picture, and also that she would have to go to Heathbury anyway if an operation was necessary. 'We simply haven't got the facilities here,' he finished.

Miss Fielding sighed and admitted defeat, but she rallied sufficiently to ask, 'Why don't they update this hospital, instead of scrapping it and building a completely new one? Then everybody would be happy.'

Emma would have liked an answer to that too, and she awaited his reply with interest.

'I think it's all tied up with needing a new hospital to replace Stonebridge. It's obviously cheaper to make the two hospitals into one. Updating can never be anything but a botched up job.'

Miss Fielding let him have the last word, but when he had gone she had a private talk with Emma.

'That young doctor is very nice, but he's typical of the modern generation. They all want to pull things down and replace them with things nobody wants. This is a much-loved little hospital and it fulfils a great need, so why can't we be allowed to keep it?'

They continued on the same lines for several minutes, with the result that when Emma's two hours off duty came she set out with her petition with renewed enthusiasm. She had resolved to go out seeking signatures every day, and when the end of the week came and she had a free Saturday she would give up the whole day to it.

It was a tiring job and—she had to admit it— sometimes a boring one. But, as the pages slowly filled, an inner sense of satisfaction spurred her on. So far she had concentrated on the older part of the town, but when she had her whole day free she decided to make a start on the new estates. Most of the inhabitants wouldn't be working on a Saturday and possibly she might find a good proportion of them at home.

She was slightly nervous as she walked up the first garden path and pressed the bell. The people living in this area might not be so wholeheartedly in favour of keeping the cottage hospital as others had been. Sounds of pop music wafted through the letterbox and eventually the door was opened by a teenage girl with a mop of fuzzy blonde hair.

'Yes?' She stared at the conventionally dressed nurse in surprise. 'If you want Mum and Dad, they're out.'

Emma rattled off the few sentences which had become part of her campaign. The girl listened without interest but languidly agreed to scrawl her signature.

'Quite honestly, I couldn't care less,' she confided.

It was not the most encouraging start but Emma quickly rallied. As she plodded on her way and the hours drifted past, her spirits rose and fell in strict proportion to the number of signatures she collected. A depressing number of people were definitely against the petition and a few even entered into an argument with her. Emma put up a spirited defence but once or twice felt she had been defeated. By lunchtime she was very much in need of cheering up.

The weather had been fine when she started but now there were grey skies and a threat of rain. Also, she was quite absurdly tired. Used to standing as she was, she had found waiting at front doors much worse than her normal routine. As she reached a short crescent, she decided to work her way along it and then go home. Here, the houses were mostly flats, and very few people seemed to be at home. She was nearly at the end when her ring at a bell produced a series of loud barks. There were footsteps in the hall and someone told the dog to belt up.

There was something familiar about his voice.

A moment later, Craig stood in the doorway, staring at her in amazement. 'Emma! What on earth are you doing here?' His eyes dropped to the clipboard in her hand. 'Oh, I see.' And before she could speak, he said crisply, 'You're surely not expecting me to sign your petition?'

There was a brief silence. Rex came forward, smelt her hand and then licked it. Recovering slightly from the shock, Emma pulled herself together.

'You might have changed your mind,' she suggested lightly.

He shook his head. 'I'm not likely to do that. I believe it's sentiment and nothing else that makes some people cling to a small out-dated hospital when they could have a grand new one a few miles further away. Mileage is no problem these days.'

'It is to some people.'

Vaguely, Emma was aware that she had sounded tired and forlorn. She was cold too, and absolutely longing for a hot drink.

Craig looked at her keenly. 'I'm sure it's time you had a break from all this. Come in and sit down for a bit. Sammy and I were just going to have some lunch. It's only bread and cheese and packet soup, but if you'll share it with us, it'll put new life into you.'

In a daze, Emma stepped into a small lobby, and was conducted to a room at the back of the flat with French windows into the garden. A gas-fired imitation log fire glowed cheerfully, and the warmth wrapped her round like a blanket. Dr Cox, wearing fawn cord trousers and a matching sweater, was setting out plates and mugs. She looked very much at home, which was more than Emma felt.

She said, 'Hi!' and automatically laid a place for a third person, but her casual acceptance of the situation did little to make Emma feel anything but an intruder.

It had been no part of her plan to call on Craig. She had known he lived in this area, but not his actual address. Even so, if she had found him alone her reaction would have been very different from what she was experiencing at the moment. The two doctors, she remembered, had been at medical school together and had been friends ever since, which would account for the intimate atmosphere she had sensed when she came in. Partly, anyway.

But, whatever Emma's private thoughts were, it was impossible not to enjoy her lunch. The soup was followed by four kinds of cheese, a great heap of granary rolls, and a wooden bowl piled high with fruit. She said very little, but conversation flowed freely between the other two, mostly on medical matters.

Eventually Dr Cox announced that it was time

she got back on her round. 'Thanks for the food, Craig, and the advice too. I really was very concerned about that patient and you've cleared the air quite a bit.'

'Any time,' he said cheerfully, and conducted her to the door.

Left alone, Emma sipped her second mug of coffee and reviewed the situation. It was obviously her duty to continue with her self-imposed task but a glance out of the window showed her that the threatened rain had now become a fact. To go on trying to collect signatures in such weather would be ridiculous.

She had come to that conclusion when Craig came breezily back.

'Feeling better now?' he asked.

'Much. You've just about saved my life.'

He grinned. 'I doubt that, but I might have prevented you developing a flourishing example of the common cold. Are you going to be sensible now and pack it in for the day?'

'I—think so.'

'Great!' He reseated himself at the table and inspected the coffee-pot. 'So what are you going to do instead?'

Emma improvised rapidly. 'I thought of going home and washing my hair.'

Craig looked at the raindrops streaming down the window. 'You could wash it in soft water if you went out in this, but I should think it would be a very uncomfortable proceeding. I can think of a lot more interesting ways of spending a free afternoon.'

'Like what?' she challenged him, meeting the

gaze of his diamond-bright eyes across the table, and then wishing she hadn't.

His smile was gently teasing. 'Like helping me with the washing-up,' he suggested airily.

Emma wasn't at all sure what she had expected—or hoped for—but it certainly hadn't been that. Nevertheless, she quickly rallied. 'Of course I'll help you—it's the least I can do.' She went out to the kitchen and turned on the hot tap. 'Let's get on with it.'

They worked quickly and almost in silence, and the job was soon done. To Emma it seemed almost unbelievable that she and Craig were doing a simple domestic task together, but she couldn't accept that it signified a step forward in their largely argumentative relationship. Making use of his unexpected visitor had merely seemed to him a good way of getting the washing-up done without having to do it by himself.

His comment at the end of it confirmed her opinion.

'Thanks, Emma. If you hadn't been here, I'm afraid the things would have had to wait until tonight—or even tomorrow.'

'I'm glad I've been some use,' she said lightly. 'Is this your day off—and I don't mean domestically?'

'Not really. I took surgery this morning and I've been on call since, but that's not such a tie now that we've all got mobile phones.' Again he looked at the weather. 'I shall have to take Rex for a walk later on so I hope it clears up.' He moved nearer and slid his hands lingeringly over her shining pleat of hair. 'You don't really want to go home and wash it, do you?'

It was the last thing she wanted to do. Her heart was urging her to stay here with Craig, just the two of them, happy together without argument—and particularly without argument about the hospital. She didn't want much more than that, not yet, but just to have that small amount of intimacy would be so wonderful.

'Your hair is so soft, just like silk,' Craig murmured. 'But I don't like it all tight like this——'

'I've got my uniform on,' she reminded him breathlessly, and just managed not to mention the petition. 'I couldn't have it hanging round my face the way I do when I'm walking on the beach.'

He was pulling the pins out and dropping them on the floor. When her hair was free, he ran both hands through it, and a slow, sensual shiver passed down her spine. Her pulses racing, Emma raised her face and unconsciously offered him her lips.

The front doorbell rang.

CHAPTER SEVEN

A GIRL with long mousy hair stood in the porch, clutching a large, limp baby. She looked no more than nineteen and was clearly in a state of acute panic.

'My baby, Doctor——' She held the child out to him. 'I think he's stopped breathing. Oh, God, I'm so frightened——'

Craig took her burden from her. 'What happened, Sheila? Did he choke? Try to tell me exactly.'

'I was giving him his dinner—he loves his food—and I thought a bit of orange would be good for him—it's vitamin C, after all. . .'

Emma had been studying the baby anxiously and she had already noticed a tiny scrap of orange fibre on his bib. At the same moment Craig inserted his little finger into the open mouth. There was a moment of tension and then he hooked out the slice of fruit which had caused the trouble. It was hardly necessary to hold the little boy upside-down and thump his back, but he did so, immediately causing an outraged yell.

'Oh, thank you, thank you, Doctor.' Sheila struggled with tears. She seized her child and hugged him. 'You've saved my Robbie's life! I shall never forget it—never!'

Craig smiled, but was quickly serious again. 'Just one thing, love, don't give him a whole

116

section of orange again until he's older. He can't cope with it, so please stick to juice for a little longer.'

'Oh, I will, I will!' Still pouring out thanks, she fled down the garden path and in through the next gate.

'It's handy sometimes, having a doctor living next door,' Craig said with a smile as they returned to the house. 'Sheila's a single parent and a good kid, and she does her best. Unfortunately her mum doesn't live near enough to help in that sort of emergency.'

Emma was feeling extraordinarily emotional. The incident had taken barely a minute but a child's life had been saved. Supposing Craig had been out! She couldn't bear to think about the possibility, yet when she said as much to him, he refused to contemplate such a catastrophe.

'I *was* at home and that's all that matters.' He slipped his arm into hers and steered her back to the living-room. 'What had you planned to do this afternoon if it hadn't rained?'

'Go on with the petition, of course,' she said firmly. 'When we were outside just now, I noticed it looked like clearing up quite soon.'

'What a conscientious girl you are!'

In actual fact, Emma was having trouble with her conscience, which was doing its best to prod her into action. Instead of being ruled by it, she was fighting back, pointing out that she had worked very hard that morning for hours and hours, and surely she deserved to take the afternoon off if Craig had anything else to suggest?

Apparently he had.

'I was hoping you'd help me to take Rex for a walk when the rain stops. In the meantime——' He broke off as the telephone rang.

Emma waited by the fire, wishing she knew how he'd intended to finish the sentence. Perhaps he'd tell her when he came back.

But instead of that he asked a question.

'Do you remember old Mr Freeman at Pember Hall Cottages? We called on him the day Ron Stapleton was thrown from his horse.'

'Of course I remember. He was bronchitic. Besides, he was a patient in the hospital not long ago.'

'That was his daughter on the line. Apparently the old chap is rather worse than usual, and she's worried because she wants to go away to look after her own daughter who's just had her first baby. She thought maybe I'd admit him to hospital for a week or so.' He paused, looking at Emma intently. 'How about coming with me to see him?'

Emma drew a deep breath and glanced at the window. It was impossible not to feel pleased that the improvement in the weather was still only a suggestion.

'I'd like to,' she said simply. 'But do you mind if I ring my mother first?' Seeing his surprise, she added hastily, 'She was expecting me back to lunch.'

'Go ahead.'

A few minutes later, when they were driving down the road in the red BMW with Rex on the back seat, Craig said abruptly, 'Do you always keep your mother informed of your every move?'

Stung by his critical tone, Emma looked at him

indignantly. 'Of course I don't. What on earth made you ask that?'

'It's happened before, that's why. It does seem to me that you rather overdo the dutiful daughter act.'

'So what?' Emma was suddenly furiously angry. 'My mother and I get on very well indeed. We're friends as well as family, and I can't see it's any concern of yours if I treat her with consideration.'

'None whatsoever,' Craig said blandly, 'but you're a big girl now, Emma dear, and it really is time you cut the apron-strings.'

'You don't know what you're talking about. It's different for a man, and you don't seem to be close to your family anyway, but I'm lucky enough to get on well with my mother, like I said, and I prefer to let her know where I am and what I'm doing.' Resisting a childish impulse to add *So there!* Emma shut her mouth firmly and glared ahead.

Craig halted before turning into the High Street. 'We're not in any particular hurry. Is there another way of getting to Pember instead of going through that labyrinth of lanes?'

Faced with an ordinary question like that, spoken in an ordinary voice, she regained her temper as suddenly as she had lost it. 'We could go by the coast road, the one that leads to the marina, and then turn inland. It's a bit further but nicer.'

Craig swung the car round the corner and down towards the sea. He was silent for a moment and then he said calmly, 'Did that explosion make you feel better?'

'I didn't need to be made to feel better,' Emma told him defensively.

'Sorry—my mistake!' He stretched out his left hand and put it briefly on hers. 'Let's forget it, shall we? In case you haven't noticed, it's stopped raining and the sun will soon be out.'

Emma was only too ready to forget what he had called her 'explosion'. She didn't really understand why she had felt that urgent need to quarrel with Craig. His criticism of her attitude towards her mother had been an excuse rather than a reason.

'It seems rum,' Craig was saying, 'that Saxham wasn't built at the mouth of the Wick instead of further along the coast. It's a very ancient town, isn't it? In the old days people liked to have a river handy for travelling inland.'

'It's all marshy around here,' Emma explained as they came in sight of the row of houseboats where the wood-carver, Michael Hammond, lived. 'It's no good for building.'

'Peter the Great managed to build St Petersburg on marshy ground, and that's a big city.'

Emma didn't want to talk about Peter the Great. Instead, she said quickly, 'Turn left here,' and Craig swung the car up a narrow muddy road leading up-river to Pember. They did not speak again until they reached the village but her thoughts were busy. Though outwardly she had regained her equilibrium, inside she still felt churned up and quite unable to forget her outburst, no matter how hard she tried. It wasn't like her to sound off over such a small matter, and she still didn't understand it.

*   *   *

It was very hot in Mr Freeman's small living-room. As before, there was a good fire in the grate and, in addition, a paraffin heater under the window. The old man looked flushed and his breathing was bad, but he greeted them in his usual caustic style.

'What you doing here, then? I didn't send for you.'

'I heard your daughter was a bit concerned——'

'You won't see Lizzie. She's gone shopping in Saxham.'

Craig approached the bed. 'You're the one I want to see, not your daughter.' He put his fingers on Mr Freeman's bony wrist. 'Hmm—a bit faster than it ought to be. Have you been getting over-excited?'

'Fat chance of that!'

The old man chuckled hoarsely and started himself coughing. Tears streamed from his rheumy eyes and he choked and spluttered. Seeing a box of tissues nearby, Emma handed him a couple, and eventually he recovered.

Craig sat down beside the bed. 'I hear you've got a great-grandchild—a little girl, isn't it?'

'So Lizzie says.'

'And since it's her daughter who's had the baby, she naturally wants to go and see them both, and stay for a few days.' He paused, but Mr Freeman remained silent. 'But she can't go unless she's sure you're being looked after properly. You wouldn't want her to be worried about you all the time she was away?'

'S'pose not.'

Craig stood up with an air of everything being

nicely sorted out. 'That's settled, then. I'll arrange for you to be moved to the hospital for a short time, and while you're there we'll see if we can do something about that cough.'

For a moment there was a rebellious expression on the wrinkled old face, and then he gave in. 'It warn't so bad last time I was there.' He glanced at Emma. 'Will you be looking after me?'

She assured him that she would—most of the time anyway—and the visit ended.

Craig unlocked the car and was greeted by Rex as though he had been gone for hours. 'I think I'll take him for a short walk round the village,' he said to Emma. 'You don't mind?'

'Of course not.' An idea leapt into her head. 'While you're doing that I'll see if I can collect some more signatures. It wouldn't take me long to cover the whole village.'

He said, 'OK,' in a carefully neutral tone, and they separated, Craig making for the lane which went towards Pember Hall and Emma heading for the nearest cottage.

It took longer than she had expected, because of the villagers' tendency to recount various hospital experiences which they and members of their family had had. They were all, it seemed, indebted in one way or another to Saxham cottage hospital, and very willing to sign the petition.

Returning triumphant, she saw that Craig was already back, and talking to someone with an old-fashioned coach-built pram, gleaming with polish. There was only one person it could possibly be, and Emma greeted Anne Stapleton with genuine pleasure. When Rosemary had been duly admired, Anne switched to the subject of the dinner party she had mentioned before leaving the hospital.

'Well, it's not really a party,' she corrected herself. 'Just the two of you. When can you come?'

'Since you're the hostess, wouldn't it be better if you fixed the date?' Craig suggested with a smile. 'Then we'll arrange to fit in with it, emergencies permitting.'

'Normally I'm not off duty until eight-thirty,' Emma said, 'but I can often make a special arrangement for occasions like this.'

Anne smiled approvingly. 'That's how things ought to be, but you wouldn't get that sort of consideration in an ordinary hospital, which is one of the reasons why I just love our dear little cottage hospital.'

Emma seized her opportunity, but she couldn't resist a glance at Craig and found him carefully avoiding her eye.

'That reminds me,' she said to Anne. 'Would you like to sign the petition I'm getting up?'

'Petition for what?'

'You know about the hospital being threatened with closure?'

'Oh, yes, I did hear something, but I hoped it was only a rumour. I was too absorbed in the baby to take much notice.' Anne looked anxious. 'You're not saying it's true?'

'I'm afraid so.' Emma plunged into a full explanation. 'So that's why I'm getting up this petition. I spent all the morning collection signatures in Saxham, and I've just got some more here.'

'I'll sign with pleasure.' Anne took the clipboard and scribbled illegibly. 'I wish you every success,' she went on, handing it back. 'Reverting to the dinner party, I'll phone you both when I've arranged a date with Ron.' She shared out a radiant smile between them. 'It's been lovely meeting you again.'

They said goodbye and Craig drove off. As they left the village, he turned his head and looked at Emma.

'It's all a waste of time, you know. Nothing ordinary people can do will alter what the NHS plans for——'

Emma interrupted him hotly. 'That's where you're wrong! There have been several cases where a public outcry has halted unpopular changes.'

'Only when it's a national protest, involving marching through the streets with banners, in London or somewhere else important. A campaign run by a handful of people in a little place like Saxham that nobody's ever heard of hasn't got a chance.' His voice softened. 'Believe me, love, you'd spare yourself a terrible disappointment if only you'd accept that.'

For one awful moment Emma's resolution was shaken, but then she stuck out her chin and tightened her lips, and called up all her natural obstinacy. She'd never forgive herself if she didn't make some attempt to stop the authorities riding roughshod over ordinary people's feelings in an important matter like this.

She was still wondering whether it was worthwhile making yet another attempt to persuade

Craig to look at it differently when they reached the coastal road and he slowed down before it began to rise to the level of the cliff-top.

'Rex hasn't had much of a walk this afternoon so, if you don't mind, I'm going to let him run on the beach for a little while. I think you've had enough exercise, so shall we find somewhere to sit?'

'Sounds like a good idea,' Emma managed to say, her heart pounding.

She followed him along a narrow path between big clumps of coarse grass. In a short time it would be sunset but at present a misty sun was adding a little warmth to the scene, and for once there was no wind. Suddenly Craig halted, and she saw he had found an upturned boat, half buried in sand and shingle. It was a long time since it had been in the sea but it made a passable seat.

'This do?' He brushed away some of the sand.

'Fine!' Emma seated herself cautiously, aware of old, splintering wood. She didn't feel very safe, and the fact that Craig had put his arm round her somehow made her even less secure.

'This seems to be the best part of the day,' he said thoughtfully.

'The weather's certainly improved,' Emma agreed.

His chuckle was very close to her ear. 'Did you really think I was talking about the weather?'

'It was a possibility.'

This time he laughed out loud, but then his arm tightened and she was conscious of his warmth and nearness in every fibre of her being. Some-how her head found a resting place against his shoulder, and slowly all the stress and strain of the day melted away, to be replaced by a feeling of utter content.

It was Rex who spoilt it.

Suddenly she felt Craig stiffen beside her, and his arm dropped so abruptly that Emma almost overbalanced. Following the direction of his gaze, she saw the dog—who had been happily chasing gulls a moment ago—limping towards them.

'He's cut his paw.' Craig jumped up and went to meet his pet, who immediately sat down and held up a paw with a pathetic expression on his face.

Blood was dripping from it and Emma, almost as concerned as the owner, also went to investigate. She saw that the pad beneath the foot had been cut and was bleeding freely.

'Must have been a piece of glass.' Craig was examining it anxiously. 'Bloody careless of someone to leave broken glass lying about on the beach.'

'Poor Rex.' Emma fondled the silky head. 'Will you have to take him to a vet, or can you handle it yourself?'

'I probably could quite easily, but he may need an injection, so I think it had better be the vet. I'm quite friendly with the local man and I'll give him a ring when I get home. In the meantime, I'll tie my handkerchief round to prevent any more dirt getting in.'

That done, they went straight back to the car. Sitting silently beside Craig, Emma looked back over the long, long day. So much had happened, she could hardly remember the beginning of it,

but the highlights were still clear in her mind.
Particularly the last one.

Anne Stapleton kept her word and her invitation
was issued within a few days. By some miracle
she had fixed on a date which suited them both.

Emma dressed with care, after spending twenty
minutes trying to decide what to wear. Her smart
dresses were all more than two years old and she
longed for something new, but didn't really think
the occasion justified it. In the end, she chose a
short brown velvet skirt teamed with an apple-
green top with long tight sleeves.

She had washed her hair and taken a lot of
trouble over her make-up and, studying herself
in a long mirror, she felt a surge of excitement.
It was so long since she had dressed up and been
called for by a man. Far too long.

Punctually at seven-fifteen Craig's car nosed its
way down the narrow Little Back Lane, and found
Emma's house. She was waiting for him with the
door ajar, and quickly slipped into the car. They
greeted each other briefly but she knew he had
noted her appearance.

'Not much sign of Staff Nurse Mayfield tonight!'
he commented as he engaged the gear.

'I should hope not,' was all Emma could think
of to say.

'It will be interesting,' Craig went on, 'to see
if your personality has changed as much as your
appearance.

Slightly nettled, she flung back at him, 'What's
that supposed to mean?'

He seemed startled at her tone. 'It was only

one of those remarks which aren't meant to be taken too seriously. Shall we begin this conversation again? It seems to have started off on the wrong foot.'

Emma was very willing and she gave him a lead. 'Have you heard anything from the consultant you transferred Miss Fielding to?'

'I had a letter this morning.' He paused as they reached the High Street and crossed it. 'He confirmed my diagnosis of cholecystitis and her gallstones will have to be removed. I'm very relieved it's not cancer of the liver, which was a possibility. The whole area was so tender it was difficult to pinpoint the trouble.' He paused again. 'You'll have to direct me through these lanes.'

She did so efficiently and told him that she and her mother often cycled through them in the summer.

'Does neither of you drive?'

'We both do, but we haven't a car at present.' Emma hesitated, wanting to tell him the truth— that they were hard up—but was held back by loyalty to her father. Eventually she decided to be honest. After all, Dr Mayfield's tangled financial affairs were no secret in Saxham.

'My father—do you remember about him being killed in a car crash?—was a very good doctor and everybody loved him, but he was no businessman and he left a lot of debts. Mum and I made up our minds to clear them all before we allowed ourselves any unnecessary luxuries.'

'You call a car a luxury? I would have thought it was a necessity.'

Emma was immediately on the defensive.

'We've done very well without it, just as we've got used to living in a small house.'

They had reached the gates of Pember Hall, and Craig made no comment.

Mr Newman, wearing a short white jacket and looking very different from the horseman or chauffeur he sometimes became, admitted them to the house and their hosts came into the hall to welcome them. Anne was looking very attractive in blue, and Ron was conventionally dressed in a dark suit from the waist up, but his plaster spoilt the effect. He was getting on very well, he told them, but absolutely longing to be properly mobile again.

'What a lovely room!' Emma exclaimed as they entered the drawing-room.

It was fragrant with early narcissi in crystal vases, and comfortable with chintz-covered furniture. There was a log fire in addition to the central heating, and long deep red curtains shut out the night.

'I like it best in the summer, because it looks out on to the rose garden,' Anne said. 'What would you like to drink?'

Emma hesitated, and Ron rattled off a long list of pre-dinner drinks. She guessed that Craig would settle for something non-alcoholic because of driving, and asked for orange juice herself. At first the conversation was jerky, but once Anne got launched on the subject of Rosemary there was no need for anyone else to say very much.

It was different when they went into the elegant dining-room, lined with family portraits, and were joined by a plump girl who was introduced as the

Norland nurse looking after the baby. The wine helped—Craig accepted a glass—and soon everyone was doing their share of keeping the conversation going.

The meal was delicious—smoked salmon pâté, pheasant with all the trimmings, and a chocolate soufflé with clotted cream. It wasn't often, Emma reflected, daring to accept a second helping, that a nurse and doctor received hospitality on this scale from grateful patients.

When the time came to say goodnight, Craig suggested driving home by the cliff road. It was a wonderfully clear night, with a full moon and stars twinkling like diamonds against the dark blue of the sky.

'It seems a pity not to stop a little while and enjoy it,' he said casually. 'The headlights are spoiling the effect.' Without waiting for a reply, he drew the car off the road.

'When I was little,' Emma said dreamily, 'I used to believe that golden path across the sea really did lead to the moon.'

Craig's arm drew her closer and he leaned his head against hers. She thrilled to the roughness of his cheek and gave a long, slow sigh.

'What was that for?' he asked softly.

'Nothing. I just felt I needed a big breath, that's all.'

After that there was no more need for words. Craig's caresses, gentle at first, soon became more demanding, but Emma made no protest. When the moon was obscured by a wandering cloud, blotting out the lovely scene they had been watching, neither of them was aware of it. Only when a few raindrops pattered against the windscreen did they open their eyes to what was happening in the world outside.

'Whatever is the time?' Emma tried to see her watch. 'Heavens! It's nearly twelve. Mum will wonder why I'm so late.'

'Surely she won't be waiting up for you?'

'No, of course not, but when two people share a very small house they're bound to take a lot of notice of each other's movements, and it's ages since I went out. . .' Her voice died away.

She had been going to say 'with a man', but changed it hurriedly to, 'in the evening'. Paul was the last man who had taken her out, the night before he went off to London with fervent promises of an early marriage, and then vanished.

With all her strength she thrust aside the memory of Paul. For too long she had mourned for him as though he had been dead—perhaps he was—and now it was time to put the past behind her and dwell in the present.

But the future still remained an unknown quantity.

CHAPTER EIGHT

RUTH was sitting at the kitchen table, drinking Horlicks. When Emma looked at her in surprise she hurried to explain.

'Please don't imagine I've been waiting up for you. I sat up late watching a play and then couldn't get to sleep. Did you have a good time?'

'Super! Gorgeous food and a lovely house. Can I have some Horlicks?'

They sat companionably at the table, sipping the warm, soothing drink and chatting desultorily. Emma couldn't help thinking what a pity it was that Craig couldn't have been an invisible witness. He didn't seem to have experienced any happy, ordinary family life, and she longed to show him some.

When they went up to bed, she was the one who couldn't get to sleep. Over and over again, she relived that magic hour or so in the car. For the first time it occurred to her that the wonderful dreamy state of bliss might be due to having been for so long starved of the attentions of a personable man. Puzzling over it, she couldn't decide whether this would be a good thing or not.

But the alternative didn't seem to be a good idea either.

She was tired in the morning, and resentful of the alarm which had faithfully roused her at six-thirty. A hot shower and a mug of coffee brought her back to a more reasonable frame of mind, and she set out to ride through a crisp, frosty morning feeling ready for anything the day might bring.

What it actually brought was an encouraging upsurge of interest in the petition.

With Miss Lenton's permission, Emma had put some ruled sheets of paper, pens and a poster on the hall table. She had to admit that the big red 'HANDS OFF OUR HOSPITAL' looked distinctly amateurish, and she was delighted when a visitor apologetically offered to do a new one.

'I used to be quite good at calligraphy when I was younger. I don't suppose I've lost the art. Are you sure you won't mind, dear?'

'I'd be thrilled! I know mine isn't at all professional, but I was never any good at art.'

'You're a good nurse and that's far more useful.' Mrs Hannay beamed at her. 'I'll bring it tomorrow when I visit my husband.'

She kept her promise, and actually brought half a dozen posters to be used in the town. Emma was greatly cheered by her help. After Craig's continued disapproval, and the lack of interest in some parts of Saxham, she had been feeling a bit depressed about her campaign.

During the week Miss Fielding returned to convalesce after her operation, and she immediately wanted to know how the petition had been faring.

'It's had a mixed reception,' Emma had to admit, 'but I'm going to press on, of course. I shall do some more canvassing at houses on my next day off, which will be on December the first.'

'You'll have to get as much done as possible before Christmas.'

Emma had realised that, but before her free day arrived something happened which put everything else out of her mind.

There was only one whole day left in November when Craig came to the hospital to visit Miss Fielding.

He did not stay long, and she had no conversation with him until, on his way out, he contrived to catch her eye so unobtrusively that she wasn't quite sure whether she had imagined it. Nevertheless, she followed him out to the landing and looked at him enquiringly.

His opening remark astounded her.

'Have you got any Scottish blood?'

'Not a drop, as far as I know. Why?' Puzzled, she looked up and unwisely met his eyes, whereupon—to her annoyance—she instantly dropped her own.

'I've got some—about a quarter—and that's why I've suddenly realised that tomorrow is St Andrew's Day.'

Emma smiled. 'I'll take your word for it. Why are you telling me all this?'

'Because, having discovered the date, I then looked around me and further found out that there's a ball at that big hotel overlooking the golf course, so I rang up and got the last two tickets. There wasn't time to ask you first.'

'Are you asking me now?' she enquired, with a lift of her eyebrows and ignoring the turmoil in her heart.

'Well, of course I am!' Craig said impatiently. 'You will come, won't you? I promise to steer you through the eightsome reel so brilliantly you'll look as though you've been doing it all your life.'

Emma was alarmed. 'There'll be Scottish dancing?'

'Oh, yes—but not very much.' He moved closer, looking down at her intently. 'You still haven't said whether you'll come.'

She thought rapidly. 'It depends on what time you want to get there. I'm not off duty until eight-thirty.'

She only had to ask Miss Lenton and no doubt she could make an arrangement which would be more convenient, yet some inner compulsion was preventing her from suggesting it. Holding her breath, she waited to see if Craig would put forward the idea himself.

Fortunately it turned out that he had evening calls to make before he would be ready to go to the ball. 'I'll call for you as soon as I can after nine o'clock. Wear your best party dress, and if it's a long one, so much the better.'

In a daze, Emma promised to do so, and avoided mentioning that she had only one evening dress and that was quite old. Paul had taken no interest in dancing. Physical fitness and photography had been his hobbies, and she had gone along with what interested him.

Surely she must have been genuinely in love?

Not stopping to search for an answer to that, Emma planned to spend her lunch-hour in the town, endeavouring to buy a long evening dress worthy of the occasion. There were some very good dress shops in Saxham. The trouble was they were also expensive.

In the end she threw economy to the winds and purchased a dress she really liked. The assistant in the shop told her she ought to wear white for a Scottish ball and produced a very simple but elegantly cut garment in soft, silky material. It had a deep plunge neckline, back and front, and clung to Emma's slender hips as though it had been made for her.

When she returned home with it that evening, her mother viewed it with amazement, and heroically refrained from making the sort of comments Emma didn't want to hear, like, 'It does seem rather expensive for a one-off occasion' or 'I do hope this young man is worth all the trouble he's put you to'.

Instead, Ruth said briskly, 'You'd better have a taxi to bring you home from the hospital. It'll be quicker than cycling and won't mess up your hair.'

'Good idea, Mum. I'll ring up and order it now.'

In the morning Emma got up extra early and washed her hair. She put everything ready for a quick change in the evening and set out for the hospital, hoping fervently that no emergencies would crop up to delay her going off duty when the time came.

The day began peacefully, and the only sour note was provided by old Mr Freeman, who was querulously asking when he could go home. Emma gave him a gentle scolding.

'You're really being very naughty. You know perfectly well your daughter's got to look after her own daughter for a little while. I'm sure she'll come back as soon as possible.' She plumped up his pillows and resettled him. 'Why don't you like it here? Most people do.'

'Don't like the meals,' he grumbled. 'All that rabbit food gives me indigestion.'

A lot of trouble was taken in the kitchen to provide a healthy diet, but quite often old-fashioned and elderly people didn't appreciate it. Concluding that it was too late to teach Mr Freeman to enjoy fibre and vitamins, Emma promised to have a word with Miss Lenton with a view to making his meals more to his liking.

The afternoon seemed endless. She had to admit she was excited—thrilled even—to be going out with Craig on such a special occasion, but at the same time she was afraid. His interest in herself meant nothing—she was sure of that— and she wished her own feelings could be as lacking in depth.

Why on earth couldn't she just accept that tonight she was partnering a very attractive man, and make up her mind to enjoy it regardless?

By eight o'clock she was beginning to look at her watch every five minutes. Time would have passed much more quickly if they had been busy, but the patients were all either watching television or quietly reading.

At twenty minutes past eight the telephone rang on the landing and Emma went to answer it. It was a paramedic speaking from the mobile phone in his ambulance.

'We'll be with you shortly, bringing a chap who had a minor crash with his car in Saxham High Street. There are no fractures as far as we can tell but he seems very confused.'

Emma replaced the handset and stood thinking. The first job was to ring Miss Lenton, who had gone over to her cottage, and then make sure there was a bed ready for the casualty. By the time he reached the hospital, the night staff would be arriving and could take charge.

There would be no need for any of the day nurses to be involved in actually nursing him until tomorrow.

The ambulance arrived within a few minutes and she went down to receive the patient with a view to dealing with the admission procedure before leaving. The two men with him were chatty and seemed puzzled about the accident.

'There was no other vehicle involved. The chap apparently drove straight into a lamp-post, but he was going slowly so nothing very drastic happened to the car. We're inclined to think he was feeling ill before the crash. He's certainly got a fever.'

Emma absorbed the information and immediately decided not to put the new arrival into a ward. In view of the word 'fever' he had better go into one of the single rooms, at least until the morning. All she could see of him at the moment was some blond hair sticking out of the usual red blanket, which told her nothing.

The ambulancemen manoeuvred their stretcher into the lift and she ran lightly up the stairs. She had collected an admission form and a chart, and was ready to meet them by the time they arrived.

It was then that she got her first look at the

patient's face, and the floor seemed to rock under her.

Surely it couldn't possibly be—it must be a chance resemblance—but the man had withdrawn a hand from beneath the blanket and was holding it out to her.

'Emma—oh, thank God you're on duty!'

She opened her mouth to say that she wasn't, but Paul went rushing on.

'I feel so hellish and I've got the most appalling headache—all I want is to crawl into bed and be looked after by you.' Sunken blue eyes gazed imploringly into her face.

'Just lie still, Paul.' It was amazing how calm her voice sounded. 'There's a room ready for you, and in no time at all you'll be settled comfortably in bed——'

'The way I feel at the moment I can't believe I'll ever be comfortable again.' His hot and shaking fingers clutched at hers. 'Can't you give me something for this bloody headache? It's been getting worse all the way from London.'

'We will, as soon as we can——' Emma broke off as Miss Lenton appeared.

Although the matron was now in charge, Paul was still clinging to her hand and she knew she must stay with him for a little while. There was no way she could hand him over to the night staff nurse and vanish.

Besides, she'd got to find out a bit more about what was happening to him. He'd always been so healthy.

She said goodnight to the ambulancemen and thanked them, and then picked up the admission form. Miss Lenton was trying to find out Paul's name but he had sunk into semi-consciousness and refused to answer.

'It's all right,' Emma said. 'I know him. He's called Paul Kennedy and he's—twenty-six.' She wrote it in quickly and then paused.

'Address?' Miss Lenton prompted.

'Sorry, I've no idea, except that it's somewhere in London.'

'Perhaps he'll be able to tell us himself tomorrow. What about next of kin?'

'I don't know that either. He has parents in the north of England, but I suppose there could be somebody in London.'

The matron was looking at her in a slightly puzzled way and Emma felt some explanation was required. 'He used to live in Saxham and—and I knew him quite well then, but we lost touch after he moved to London.'

'I see.' Miss Lenton looked down at the patient, who was lying with eyes closed. There was a hectic flush on his cheeks and his breathing was noisy. 'He doesn't seem to have forgotten you, anyway. It's a pity you're just going off duty.'

Emma hesitated. 'You think he's seriously ill, don't you?'

'I believe he might be.'

She thought of how much she had been looking forward to going with Craig to the ball, of the lovely dress waiting for her at home, and of how angry he would be—rightly—if she stood him up. She also remembered that Paul had treated her very badly indeed and she owed him nothing.

Nevertheless she heard herself saying quietly,

'I could stay on for a while if you think it would help.'

Miss Lenton seemed surprised. 'That's very good of you, my dear. I have a strong feeling that this young man will need to be specialled tonight, and we certainly have no one else available. In the meantime, I'll go and ring for a doctor. It would be most inadvisable to wait until the morning.'

Who would it be? Emma wondered. Not Craig, who had said nothing about being on call. The thought of him reminded her that she should tell him at once what had happened, and then there was her mother. She would be getting anxious.

At that moment, Maggie Dereham, the night staff nurse, looked in. 'You still here, Emma? If you aren't in a rush to get off, I'd be glad if you'd help me get this chap properly into bed. My assistant's busy with bedtime drinks.'

Emma nodded. 'OK, but I must make some phone calls first. I won't be long.'

She rang her mother first, as that was likely to be a short call, provided she only said someone was very ill and mentioned no name. Craig was a different matter. She had to give him a proper explanation, and what he would make of it she dared not think.

Ruth was commendably calm. She said only, 'I'll expect you when I see you, then.'

Emma dialled Craig's number with nervous fingers. Would he understand? Looking at it from his point of view, she felt very doubtful.

'It's me—Emma.' She tried to speak naturally but her voice quivered. 'I'm terribly sorry but I haven't been able to get away from the hospital yet—an emergency has been brought in——'

'There's a night nurse, isn't there?' he demanded.

'Oh, yes, but she needs help. The case may need specialling. . .'

There was a tiny pause, and then Craig exploded. 'Let me get this straight, Emma. Are you telling me you'll be late? Or aren't you coming at all?'

Until that moment she hadn't known that her mind was made up. She had conned herself into thinking she could stay for a time and then slip away—that they might perhaps get to the ball at—say—ten o'clock. Now she saw that she owed it to Craig to make a firm decision.

'I can't ask you to wait for me indefinitely——'

He interrupted her angrily. 'This is ridiculous, Emma! You've done a full day's work and you're entitled to your time off. You're already late and you should insist on leaving now. All you've got to do is tell Miss Lenton you've got a date and must get away. She's living on the spot and can easily do a bit of overtime herself.'

'I—I would if the patient didn't happen to be someone I used to know. He's very ill and seems to think I'll be looking after him.' Emma drew a deep breath and waited for another explosion.

It didn't come. At first there was silence at the other end, and then Craig said frostily, 'I have a strong feeling it's that guy you used to be in love with—the one who went off and left you high and dry. Am I right?'

'Yes—yes, it is. Oh, Craig, I'm so disappointed!' Emma stopped to struggle with a lump in her throat. 'Do please try to understand and forgive me.'

He gave her no indication that he might do either. Instead he said curtly, 'I'm afraid it's beyond me to analyse your motives at the moment, but no doubt they're quite clear to you. Am I right in thinking you've decided not to come at all?'

'I think that would be best,' she faltered. 'As I said, I can't keep you waiting indefinitely and—and I may not be able to get away for ages.'

'If that's your decision, we now know exactly where we are. I think I'll see if Sammy Cox will come in your place. Might as well salvage something from this muddle.' He was suddenly hurtfully sarcastic. 'I'm sure you'd like to be able to care for your—friend without having to concern yourself with having stood me up in order to do so.'

Turning rather blindly away from the phone, Emma found a pre-nursing student who was Maggie's assistant hovering near by. 'What is it, Beth?' she asked drearily.

'There's a taxi-man outside, Staff. Says he can't wait any longer. . .'

'Heavens! I'd completely forgotten the taxi.' Emma dived into the locker-room and retrieved her handbag. She found a five-pound note and held it out. 'Give him this, please, Beth. It ought to be plenty but don't forget the tip.'

Back in Paul's little room, she found he had his eyes open.

'I thought you'd left me,' he murmured fretfully. 'You won't do that, will you, Emma?'

Maggie had begun to undress him, and she kept her face so remarkably blank that Emma could guess at her surprise without difficulty.

Stifling her own feelings, she ignored Paul's question and said cheerfully, 'The doctor will be here soon, and when we know what's wrong with you we'll be able to get busy making you feel better.'

He was silent for a moment and she thought he was sinking back into semi-consciousness. Then he looked up into her face and she saw fear in his clouded eyes.

'It can't just be flu, can it? I've never been like this before.' He paused, visibly struggling for the strength to continue. 'I've felt odd all day. . .'

'What sort of odd?' Working automatically with Maggie, Emma eased him out of his shirt.

'Headachy, and then my neck began to feel stiff, but it wasn't very bad until I was more than halfway to Saxham, and by then it seemed best to go on.'

'I think it probably was.'

Emma had spoken truthfully, but the pang which shot through her was like a knife-thrust in her heart as she thought of the cost to herself of Paul's mysterious illness.

As Miss Lenton came in with Dr Roberts, Maggie slipped away to get on with her other duties. Emma retired to the background and watched intently as the doctor made a slow and careful examination.

'I'd like to do a lumbar puncture,' he said when he had finished, giving the patient a friendly smile.

'It won't hurt, but I'm afraid you'll have to sit up while it's done. Don't try to move at present, though—Nurse has to fetch various items first.'

Considerably disturbed, but glad to have something to do, Emma left the room and went in search of what was required. Carefully ticking off her mental list, she added a local anaesthetic and arranged everything neatly on a sterile tray, covering it finally with a sterile cloth.

Between them, she and the matron raised Paul into a sitting position, but he was so limp it was clear he would have to be supported. As she put her arm round him and held him against her, she was conscious of a wave of emotion. The last time he and she had been in such intimate contact had been when they said goodbye before he left Saxham.

What did she feel now?

Looking desperately for the truth, trying to be objective, she found nothing sexual in that emotion, and certainly no love. She had given up a precious evening with Craig primarily because she was a nurse and Paul needed her. The feeling she was experiencing now was maternal.

But would she have been so sacrificial if he had been a stranger?

Miss Lenton had pulled up the hospital pyjama jacket and was rubbing cotton wool soaked in anaesthetic over the spot at the base of the spine where Dr Roberts would insert his needle. It was a delicate job and had to be done with immense care. His gloved hand moved cautiously until he was sure he had found the exact spot between two vertebra, and then he plunged the needle in.

There was a moment's pause before he withdrew it, filled with the required specimen of spinal fluid.

'I'll get this off to the path lab at Heathbury as soon as possible,' he said quietly to Miss Lenton as she escorted him from the room.

Emma, mechanically straightening the bedding and making her patient comfortable, knew what the doctor was afraid might have struck Paul. Meningitis. He had all the symptoms, but only analysis of the specimen could confirm the diagnosis.

She felt strangely calm and detached, and at the same time very thankful that she had responded to his appeal and stayed on.

Miss Lenton returned and told her that Dr Roberts wanted a drip set up. 'He doesn't think we should wait for the report from Heathbury before starting antibiotics——' She broke off and stared at Emma. 'Good heavens! I had quite forgotten you aren't supposed to be on duty. You'd better get off home now and I'll fix the drip myself.'

Emma hesitated, her gaze on Paul's face where he lay back against his pillows with closed eyes. 'I expect you'd like to have this patient specialled?' she asked quietly. 'It's my day off tomorrow so I could stay for the night if you like. I don't see how it can be managed any other way.'

'My dear girl. . .' Miss Lenton sounded quite moved. 'You really are a dedicated nurse. Are you sure you don't mind? It would certainly be an immense help.'

'I don't mind.' Emma's voice was steady but her smile was strained.

The harm had been done now. She had let Craig down and he probably wouldn't forgive her. She might as well make herself useful.

Time passed slowly. Apart from being watchful, checking the drip, and filling in the chart every half-hour, there was little to do and plenty of time for thinking. Inevitably Emma's mind dwelt in the past.

She had so many memories of Paul. They had met on the beach, just as she had met Craig, but without the drama. It had been summer and they had both just enjoyed a swim. It had been the most natural thing in the world to get into conversation. She had learnt that he was in a local bank but hoped to be moved to a larger branch before long. Their friendship had developed rapidly and turned to love, and until Paul had been transferred rather suddenly to London everything had been perfect.

She had missed him so much, and then, almost immediately after his departure, there had come the horror of her father's death.

And now Paul was back again, and she had no idea why.

At one o'clock Maggie came in and suggested Emma went to the dining-room for a meal. Although she wasn't hungry, she was tired and stiff from sitting, and welcomed the break. When she had swallowed as much ham and salad as she could manage, she felt a sudden yearning for fresh air.

It was very dark outside, and so still that she could hear, very faintly, the sound of the sea drifting over the sleeping town. Emma drew a slow, deep breath and longed for the relief of an outburst of tears.

As she struggled for control another sound caught her attention. A car was coming up the drive. Motionless by the front steps, she awaited its arrival, not daring to hope, yet quite unable to stop herself doing so.

The car came within the range of the porch light and drew up with a swish of gravel, and she saw that it was a red BMW.

Craig got out and came towards her. He was wearing a dinner-jacket with a bright green bow tie and matching cummerbund.

'Emma!' He came to a halt before her. 'What on earth are you doing here?'

'I could ask you the same,' she managed to reply, in quite an ordinary sort of voice. 'I would have expected you to be home and in bed by now.'

'The ball has only just finished and we stayed to the end.'

'Dr Cox was able to go with you? I'm so glad.'

'It was very good and I'm sorry you missed it.' Craig took a step nearer. 'You haven't told me why you're still here.'

They were talking like two acquaintances, and Emma didn't feel she could bear it any longer. Nevertheless, she ploughed on.

'I don't think you should find it hard to guess why. I'm specialling a very ill patient.'

'The new admission we were discussing earlier?' His voice was grim. 'No doubt he's also responsible for my presence. When I got home I found a message on my answering-machine, asking me to look in at the hospital before I went to bed. It was from Dr Roberts, and he thinks your friend may have meningitis, as you no doubt know.' He paused, but when Emma said nothing he added more gently, 'You'd better lead me to him.'

When they reached Paul's room, Maggie was filling in the chart. She glanced at Craig with some surprise and then turned to Emma.

'He came to just now and asked where you were, I said you'd be back in a minute.'

Emma made no comment, but she knew Craig had heard, though his face was inscrutable.

He spent some time studying the chart, and asked a number of questions which she answered as best she could. When he had finished he went out into the corridor and Emma followed him.

'I'm almost certain it's meningitis of the bacterial type, but we can't take it for granted. I expect Dr Roberts will be looking in during the morning but I assume you won't be here then.' He paused, looking at her intently. 'As it is, I don't understand your being allowed to work at night after a full day. It seems a little—unusual, even in these rather—er—exceptional circumstances.'

Stung by his tone, Emma tilted her chin. 'Another nurse was obviously needed and I was on the spot. Tomorrow is my day off and I shall be able to catch up with sleep then. I'd meant to get on with the petition but——' She shrugged and left the sentence unfinished.

'It's most irregular, and would never happen in a bigger hospital,' Craig said dogmatically.

'Well, of course it wouldn't!' she flung back at him.

He ignored her show of spirit and his hand rested gently and briefly on her shoulder. 'I'm off now, Emma. I hope you'll get through the night without any sort of crisis occurring. Don't hesitate to ring for help if you're worried.'

She nodded, and watched him striding down the corridor with a heavy heart. Once or twice lately she had dared to hope that something very beautiful and precious had begun to grow between them, but now it seemed to her that Paul's disastrous return had killed it dead.

A low moan from the room alerted her. Squaring her shoulders, Emma went back to the bedside, and again assumed the burden which fate had so cruelly placed upon her.

CHAPTER NINE

By MORNING Paul was even more deeply comatose, which made it easier for Emma to go off duty but added nothing to her peace of mind. Miss Lenton had conjured up from somewhere a retired nurse, who was fat and apparently placid, and quite willing to take charge of the case during the daytime. Her name was Miss Evans and she belonged to a generation which didn't use Christian names.

'Now, you get off home,' she instructed Emma briskly, 'and mind you get a good long sleep or you won't be good for much tonight. When I hand over a case, I like to know the patient's going to be properly looked after.'

So she was expected to remain on night duty? Emma sought out Miss Lenton and asked about it.

'I'm sorry, Emma.' The matron smoothed her immaculate grey hair and raised worried eyes from the reports she was studying. 'I can't at the moment see any way round the problem except by changing your normal duty time temporarily. It means we'll have only one staff nurse on day duty for a short time but I shall lend a hand as much as possible. I did think of borrowing somebody from Stonebridge but I happen to know they've got an epidemic of flu there——'

'It's all right, Miss Lenton,' Emma put in. 'I was half expecting it anyway.'

'Thank you, dear. I wish everybody had your

dedicated approach to nursing.' She smiled wanly. 'We have also to consider the matter of infection if meningitis is confirmed. With normal precautions, I don't think you are likely to be in any danger, but I must ask you not to go into the wards. I've already told Staff Nurse Dereham to keep away from Mr Kennedy's room. How is he this morning?'

Emma sighed. 'Not too good. He had a restless night and his temperature's gone up to nearly forty-one degrees.'

'That's high for the morning.' Miss Lenton pursed up her lips. 'I do wish we had a next of kin to contact. Are you sure you can't think of anyone? I believe you said you were acquainted with the patient.'

'I'm afraid I'd completely lost touch with him.'

'We could, of course, ask for the help of the police but it's far too soon for that. In the meantime, we can only go on as we're doing at present—and that means you must hurry off home and get some sleep.'

Emma was beginning to feel dazed and she was glad to escape into the cold morning air. She found her mother anxiously awaiting her at home.

'So you're back at last, dear! What on earth is going on? All I know is that you've had to look after a seriously ill patient and consequently didn't go to the ball—and I must say I think it's outrageous you should be expected to do that after working all day——'

Emma interrupted wearily. As briefly as possible, she went through the whole story.

'Are you actually saying that *Paul* is responsible for all this?' Ruth gasped.

'I'm afraid so.'

'But you don't owe him anything, Emma—he treated you disgracefully—and now you're telling me he's come back and apparently expects you to pick up the pieces——'

'You've got it all wrong, Mum—I agreed to help Miss Lenton out as much as anything.' Emma collapsed into a chair at the kitchen table. 'I'm sorry—I can hardly think straight just now—can we leave it for the present?'

Her mother so rarely lost her cool that she had been unprepared for this onslaught and it seemed the last straw. Dismissing all thoughts of breakfast, she struggled to her feet again.

'I'll go straight to bed, if you don't mind.' At the door she paused, looking back. 'By the way, I'm going on duty again tonight so will you call me at the usual time, please?'

Up in her room, her first thought was for the beautiful ballgown she had squandered so much money on. There was no sign of it. Her mother must have put it somewhere out of sight, and for that Emma was grateful.

Tired as she was, at first she found sleep elusive. Over and over again her weary mind went through the events of the last twelve hours, and as she struggled to analyse her emotions at seeing Paul again she was relieved to find they remained largely maternal. He had always made demands on her sympathy as well as her love.

It was when she began to think about the immediate future that she felt totally confused, and no amount of speculation produced any comfort. There was, she knew, a strong possibility that Paul might die, but she refused to consider that. He was young and normally very healthy. He mustn't be *allowed* to die.

It was in a much calmer frame of mind that Emma reached the hospital that evening. Her mother had also calmed down and they had had a long talk which had ended in both of them agreeing to take each day as it came.

'He's holding his own,' Miss Lenton said in answer to her anxious enquiry. 'Dr Roberts was here this morning and Dr Norbury came in this afternoon. They both said the illness was running its course, but it's much too early to assume anything.'

'Has meningitis been confirmed?'

'Oh, yes, indeed, so all the precautions we mentioned yesterday will have to be adhered to.' She looked at her watch. 'You're in good time, Emma, but I expect Miss Evans will be glad to be relieved. What an excellent woman she is! One of the old school.'

The day nurse was sitting by the window, knitting some anonymous garment in dark grey wool. She greeted Emma calmly, finished the row and put her possessions away in a bulging holdall.

'Not much change, I see.' Emma unhooked the chart and studied it.

Miss Evans glanced at the patient before replying. He appeared to be asleep.

'He's been very dopey all day, but that's to be expected. The intravenous feeding is helping him to keep his strength up, and with that and the antibiotics there should be an improvement in a day or two.' She got up stiffly. 'I hope you have a quiet night, and I'll see you again tomorrow.'

Emma went up to the bed and smoothed Paul's fair hair back from his forehead. She said softly, 'Hello there! I'm going to look after you again tonight.'

His lashes fluttered, and suddenly she found herself staring into his bewildered eyes.

'Emma?'

'Yes, it's me.' As he made a vague movement with his hand, she put her own over it and felt the heat which still consumed his body. At the same time she noticed a rash on his neck and chest. 'Is there anything I can do for you, Paul?'

'Just stay with me—you weren't here last time I woke up.'

'I was here all night,' she reminded him gently, 'and then I went home to have a sleep. I'm going to stay now.'

He had already drifted away again and Emma sat down to wait until it was time for the next check of temperature, blood pressure and respirations. A few minutes later, Miss Lenton looked in and beckoned her into the corridor. She was holding a small overnight bag.

'I've got Mr Kennedy's luggage here. The paramedics gave it to me yesterday and I put it away in that storeroom where we keep patients' possessions.' She smiled in slight embarrassment. 'I'm afraid I then forgot all about it. It really is time I retired!'

Emma took the holdall with mixed feelings. She

hated the thought of examining Paul's possessions—it seemed a violation of his privacy when he was too weak to protest—and it was very unlikely that the bag would contain anything except overnight requirements.

She put off opening it—adjusting the drip, making the half-hourly check, tidying the bedding. Then she propped the door open and undertook her task in the corridor, just in case he should come to and be disturbed by what she was doing.

Pyjamas, a small quantity of clean shirts, underwear and socks, a thick black sweater and toilet articles. It was just as she had expected.

Making sure there was nothing else, Emma slid her fingers into a small pocket which appeared at first to be empty. Inside she found a passport-sized photograph of a girl with corn-coloured hair cut with a fringe, and a pretty, smiling face. Across the bottom of it was scrawled, 'All my love.'

Intrigued, Emma stared at it for some time, wishing it could give her the information she needed, but the girl stared back, smiling and presenting Paul with all her love, but offering no other information.

How much did it mean to him?

In his present state it was impossible to ask, however tactfully, and no one knew when—if ever—he would recover sufficiently for questioning.

By the fourth evening Miss Evans's knitting had grown considerably and Emma suspected it might

be a sweater. Not for herself, surely? She was big
enough without that sort of garment.

As she waited in the corridor for the elderly
nurse to join her for what had become a routine
nightly report, she reflected that these days her
thoughts—apart from those concerning her nursing—seemed to consist mostly of trivial items like
that. She had the odd feeling she was living in a
vacuum, and the only reality was here in this small
room where Paul lay half-in and half-out of
a coma.

'He's been a little better today,' Miss Evans
announced, 'and I think he'll pull through. I pride
myself on not letting my patients die and I've
worked hard on your young man.'

'He's not my young man,' Emma protested, but
she might as well not have bothered.

'Then why's he always got your name on his
lips?' Miss Evans demanded. 'He talked a lot
when his fever was at its height and it was quite
obvious you meant a great deal to him.'

'I used to know him very well when he lived
in Saxham but that was ages ago.' Emma set her
lips firmly and defied her colleague to probe any
further.

The elderly nurse directed a shrewd look at her
from a pair of sharp blue eyes but did not pursue
the matter. 'Miss Lenton rang the police today,'
she said instead. 'Nobody's reported our man
missing, but they put his name on their list in case
somebody turns up looking for him.' She tucked
her holdall under her arm and set off down the
corridor. 'Night-night. See you tomorrow.'

On the point of disappearing, she remembered

something. 'None of the doctors has been in today—not yet anyway.'

Emma went into the room and found Paul awake. He was looking at her with a gleam of intelligence in his eyes, and he even found sufficient strength to hold out his hand to her. Taking it in her own, she realised it was considerably less hot. With a great wave of thankfulness she admitted he really was better.

What the result for herself might be, when he was fully recovered, she had no idea, but it was impossible not to rejoice.

'Is it night again already?' he asked in his weak voice. And when she confirmed it, he managed to add, 'I've been asleep an awful lot lately and that makes me muddled about the time.'

'You're better this evening,' Emma told him, smiling into his eyes.

Paul was silent for a moment, still holding her hand. 'Have I been very ill?' he asked eventually.

'You certainly were for a day or two.' Emma hesitated. 'Do you remember anything about it?' Holding her breath, she waited for his reply.

'Just odd bits. Like driving along the High Street and feeling ghastly——' He broke off, frowning, and then winced as his head reminded him of the severe pain he had been suffering.

Emma scolded herself for allowing her burning desire to know more to get the better of her nursing instincts. 'Never mind,' she said quickly. 'It will all come back when you're stronger.'

Suddenly she realised that the door, which she had left ajar, had been pushed open and someone was looking into the room. Glancing over her shoulder, she saw that it was Craig. All her instincts were urging her to snatch her hand out of Paul's grasp; instead of that, she released it very gently and turned to greet Craig with all the composure she could summon.

His face was utterly without expression. He was cool, courteous, and very much the doctor visiting a patient whom he scarcely knew. His 'Good evening' was quiet, and might have been addressed to either of them. Neither answered it. With no further attempt to communicate just then he picked up the chart and studied it intently.

Emma retired to the background and stood with her hands behind her. Outwardly her composure matched Craig's but inwardly she was almost seething. If only he hadn't come in just at that moment! He was bound to misinterpret those linked hands.

He finished with the chart and tidily returned it to its hook, then stood for a moment looking down at the patient, whose eyes were again closed.

'Quite an improvement,' he observed, moving away towards the door. 'Is the rash troubling him?'

Emma followed him. 'A little.'

'Some soothing cream should help. No doubt Miss Lenton can supply it. Otherwise continue with the drip but reduce the nourishment he's receiving through it and tomorrow he can be introduced to a light diet, provided he's able to tolerate it. It's important to go very slowly.'

Emma swallowed a desire to murmur, Yes,

Doctor, in a meek voice, and contented herself with nodding.

For the first time Craig really looked at her, but he might just as well not have bothered for she couldn't read his expression. He said quietly, 'Goodnight, Emma,' in a bleak sort of voice and departed.

As she went back into the room, there came a murmur from the bed. 'Not a very friendly bloke.'

'He certainly wasn't this evening,' Emma said with feeling. 'Would you like to settle for the night now?'

Paul was tired after so much rational talking and fell into a deep, restful sleep. He woke early and, for the first time, Emma made him a cup of tea. Propped up with numerous pillows, he managed a few sips with her help to steady the feeding-cup.

Suddenly he held up an arm in its faded blue stripes. 'Why on earth am I wearing these awful pyjamas? What's happened to my own?'

'You've remembered that you had some?'

'Of course I did!' he exclaimed impatiently. 'I had a suitcase, didn't I?' His face changed and he brushed a hand over his forehead. 'No, it wasn't a suitcase. I brought my old airline bag. Where is it?'

'Right here in this room.' Emma put a hand on his shoulder. 'Don't try to look round—I expect your neck is still stiff. Lie still and I'll get it for you.' She picked up the bag which was standing against the wall next to his locker.

Although she sounded completely calm, her pulses had quickened. It could be that she was about to learn a great deal more about Paul and she longed to bombard him with questions. Instead of that, she went very slowly indeed.

'We didn't have your luggage at the beginning so we had to put you into hospital pyjamas. Then, when it turned up, you were far too ill to be bothered with being changed into your own clothing. It might have triggered off memories you weren't ready for. We knew you'd remember everything eventually.'

Had that moment come?

'That makes sense,' Paul said weakly, 'but I think I would like to change now.'

It took a long time because Emma seized the opportunity to give him a more thorough wash than had been possible hitherto. At the end of it she was not surprised to find him too exhausted for any further delving into his memory. She was obliged to go off duty without learning even whether he had remembered the photograph.

It was quite possible that the girl had become so unimportant to him that he had forgotten her picture was in his holdall.

She had to wait another twenty-four hours before finding out what she so desperately needed to know.

When she came on duty that evening, she was disappointed to find Paul obviously tired and disinclined for conversation, though she had a feeling he was doing a lot of thinking.

It was different in the morning. He woke early, as he had done the previous day, and drank a whole cup of tea. Studying him unobtrusively, Emma felt that she was seeing for the first time Paul the man, and not the desperately ill patient.

Eventually he said slowly, 'Have you ever wondered what brought me to Saxham?'

Emma got a grip on herself. 'Once or twice,' she admitted casually. 'Are you going to tell me?'

Instead of answering the question, he asked her to hand him his bag. When she had done so, he immediately slid his fingers into the pocket and drew out the photograph. He stared at it for so long that Emma's patience ran out.

'What a pretty girl!' She drew a long, steadying breath. 'Who is it?'

He held it out to her and, taking it in her hand, she studied the attractive face she had seen before—but she wasn't about to tell him that.

'My wife,' Paul told her, and there was a sadness in his voice which alarmed her in spite of her overwhelming relief.

'What's her name?' she found herself asking with commendable calm.

'Jill.'

Once more Emma had to wait. The conversation had come to a full-stop and Paul was looking so tired that she felt concerned for him. Perhaps she shouldn't have questioned him like this? Maybe he wasn't yet up to it?

Yet, having started, she felt she had to go on. If he didn't unburden himself now he would go on thinking about it all day and that would do him no good at all.

'We all thought it strange that no one had reported you missing. Miss Lenton rang the police, but they knew nothing about you.'

The information obviously startled him. 'I didn't know that. Being reported to the police makes me feel like a criminal.'

Emma tried to lighten the conversation. 'Your only crime was getting ill! She phoned because we were afraid someone might be missing you.' She paused. 'Your wife, for instance.'

A bitter expression crossed Paul's ashen face. 'I don't know if Jill is missing me or not. We had a terrible row and she stormed out.' He frowned, thinking deeply. 'That was in the morning. I'd already rung up the bank and reported sick, and— and suddenly I made up my mind to drive to Saxham and see you.'

Emma wanted to say angrily, I don't know how you had the nerve after disappearing without a word more than two years ago, but he was still too ill for that sort of recrimination and she controlled herself.

She said instead, 'So you were already feeling ill when you left London? It really was a crazy thing to do!'

Paul wasn't listening. 'My car—what happened to it? I still can't remember the accident at all clearly.'

'It's at a local garage. There wasn't much damage but they've had to wait until you got better before they could do anything about it.'

'At this moment I can't imagine ever wanting to drive again.' He sighed heavily. 'I don't seem to have the strength of a kitten.'

'You'll soon start feeling stronger,' Emma told him, suddenly turning into a nurse again. 'You're making very good progress, as a matter of fact, and I think that's because you were so fit.'

He closed his eyes and appeared to slip into a

doze. Leaving him to rest, Emma went over to the window. She needed time to recover from what had been a difficult and emotional conversation for her too. Now that she knew Paul was married, she was no longer afraid he had come back to begin all over again with herself. A blazing row didn't mean the marriage was over. Jill was probably at home again and desperately worried by his disappearance.

Then why hadn't she phoned the police?

Staring out into the darkness, and seeing nothing except her own reflection, she debated how to approach the next step. Somehow she had to get an address out of him—or, better still, a telephone number—so that his wife could be contacted.

But supposing she wasn't there? It had to be admitted that she might not be, and the effect on Paul could be serious in his present weak state.

Returning to the bed, she decided to approach the matter from a different angle. When he opened his eyes, she deliberately made her tone businesslike.

'At least we now know who your next of kin is. Matron's been worrying because the hospital records couldn't be filled in properly.'

Paul smiled faintly. 'Red tape?'

'Exactly. So would you mind giving me the gen?'

He spelt out his address very slowly and carefully, and then Emma waited patiently while he tried to remember his phone number. This proved more difficult, but at last she had it and she put the precious piece of paper carefully in her breast pocket. That done, she looked at her watch. Seven-thirty.

If Jill was at home, she might leave for work—assuming she had a job—before Miss Lenton arrived and made the call. Wouldn't it be better to ring now?

Her mind made up, Emma said casually, 'I'll just go along to the office and leave a note for Miss Lenton. You can have another little nap while I'm gone.'

She met no one on the way, and when she got there closed the door firmly behind her. Her hands were trembling as she dialled the number. It was so desperately important that Jill should have got over the row and returned home. Even though Paul had treated her—Emma—so badly, she still wanted him to be happy.

The phone rang for a long time, but at last it was lifted at the other end. A faint 'Hello' reached her, and she suddenly realised she hadn't rehearsed what she was going to say.

'Is that Jill Kennedy?' The faint voice confirmed it and Emma hurried on. 'You don't know me, but I live at Saxham and I'm a nurse——'

'Saxham?' The voice was much stronger now, and full of astonishment. 'If you want to speak to Paul, I'm afraid he's not here just now.'

'I know.' Emma took a deep breath. 'I've got a very great——' She had been going to say 'shock' but altered it to 'surprise for you'. Rapidly, before Jill could interrupt, she gave a brief account of what had been happening to her husband.

'Meningitis! But people die of that——'

'Paul's making a good recovery.'

'Oh, thank God!' Jill swallowed an audible sob. 'Did you say you're a nurse? I can believe what you say, then.'

'I wouldn't mislead you on such an important matter. I expect you've been wondering where he was——'

'You can say that again! I went to see my mum for a few days and only got back last night. I've been made redundant, you see, and Paul was upset about it—he seemed to think it was my fault. Anyway, we had a row.' There followed a full description, and then, 'When can I come and see him?'

Emma gave her careful details of the complicated journey from London to Saxham by train. Jill would be able to take the Intercity as far as Heathbury, and then change to a little local train which she would have to leave at Stonebridge, afterwards transferring to a bus.

It was all written down carefully at the other end, which took some time. Emma was about to end the conversation when Jill started off again.

'I'm so grateful to you for ringing me up. I really was desperately worried. I shall come and visit Paul as fast as I can get there—I just don't know how I'm going to wait. You see, I've got something to tell him.'

Emma sensed that she was on the verge of spilling the news to herself, and hastily ended the call. Whatever Jill had to say to her husband—perhaps she had already got a grand new job—he should be the one to hear about it first.

As she went slowly back to his room, lost in

thought, she felt thankful that he apparently hadn't told his wife about the girlfriend he had abandoned at Saxham. That would certainly have complicated their reunion.

If only Craig hadn't known about it either, he would never have put such a wrong interpretation on the situation when he had found them holding hands.

CHAPTER TEN

IT WAS two weeks before Paul was well enough
to go home, but long before that he had no need
of special nurses.

'You must take a few days off, Emma,' Miss
Lenton said. 'We can manage without you for a
little longer.'

Emma wasn't sure she wanted a break, though
at the same time she felt she needed one. The
eight nights she had spent caring for Paul had
been traumatic, to say the least. For him they had
ended happily, though in spite of his temporarily
weakened state. He was reconciled with his wife
and, in addition, Jill's news thrilled them both.
She had discovered she was pregnant.

In Emma's case, things were very different. The
invisible barrier between herself and Craig was
still there. After she stopped nursing Paul she
would scarcely see him, though she knew she had
only to take a walk on the beach at the right
time and they would probably meet. Somehow
she didn't think she could bring herself to do that.

'My days off will give me a chance to get on with
the petition,' she told Miss Lenton. 'I've hardly
touched it while I've been nursing every night.'

'You really think you're making progress?'

'Oh, yes.' Emma forced herself to sound
enthusiastic. The pessimism she had encountered
among certain people had been getting her down,

in spite of her determined optimism. 'I thought I'd carry on until a few days before Christmas, but wait until the holiday is over before taking the lists to Heathbury. I daren't wait any longer, because once they've fixed on a site I don't think there'll be much hope.'

Miss Lenton's expression said only too clearly that she feared there wasn't much anyway, but she said nothing.

On the morning before she was due to start working on days again, Emma awoke to find the weather had turned unusually mild for December. Leaning out of her bedroom window, she drew in a deep breath of sea air and felt a great longing to take a walk along the beach instead of tramping pavements. If she postponed her outing until the middle of the morning she would be very unlikely to meet Craig, and even if she did meet him, would it matter all that much?

They could surely behave like two ordinary human beings, who knew each other moderately well but had no deeper feelings.

Her mother applauded the plan. 'I'd come with you if I didn't have to go to the nursery school. Why don't you walk as far as the marina? It will do you all the good in the world.'

Emma needed more than that to do her good, but she smiled and agreed.

In spite of her inner depression, she felt a superficial enjoyment as she crunched along. The sea was calm and the tiny waves broke gently on the pebbles. The sun, though slightly veiled with mist, was as warm as though it were spring. She passed the place where the two boys had tried to make a cave and noted that recent heavy rain and another fall of sand had obliterated all signs of their work.

Gradually the distant marina became larger and clearer, and at last she came to the patch of rough ground where the cliffs ended. This was where she and Craig had perched on an upturned boat, and that meant she had nearly reached the towpath where the houseboats were.

A man was coming along the path, his dog bounding in front of him, and as Emma halted in consternation Rex saw her and barked. The next moment he came rushing to greet her and plant muddy paws on her jeans.

Emma stroked his black head. 'What are you doing here so far from home?'

'I could ask you that,' Craig said, arriving in the wake of his dog. 'This is much farther than you usually walk.'

She explained that she had had a few free days, but made no mention of the reason for her short holiday, and he told her it was his day off.

'I've been to see that carver chap we rescued from a diabetic coma some time ago.'

'A long time ago.' And a lot had happened since.

'It certainly seems like it. Anyway, I remembered his beautiful painted birds and booked a couple for Christmas presents.'

'Is he looking after himself properly now?'

'I think so. That narrow escape he had probably gave him a fright.'

The conversation laboured to a halt and Emma tried to think of something else to say. If they were going to walk all the way back together, they would need plenty of topics.

'Has Rex quite got over his wounded paw?' she asked as they began to trudge over the shingle.

'Isn't it obvious?' Craig smiled. 'He races about like a two-year-old when he gets the chance, but he'll be nine at Christmas.'

'I would never have thought he was as old as that. Have you had him all the time?'

'Oh, no—nine years ago I was still a student. He belonged to my parents, but when they got divorced, and both intended to re-marry, nobody seemed to want him so I took him on. I've never regretted it, even though it's sometimes difficult to fit in his needs with my work.'

Emma would have liked to offer to take Rex for a walk occasionally, but the words stuck in her throat and she talked about the weather instead. By the time they reached the steps she was getting desperate. It had never been like this before with herself and Craig—this awful constraint seemed to strangle all attempts at naturalness.

Passing Miss Mayfield's house gave them a little more material but it was a relief when they reached the High Street and their ways separated.

As she turned towards Little Back Lane, it seemed to Emma to be painfully symbolic.

Two days before Christmas, Emma put the petition away in a safe place and, temporarily, out of her mind.

Neither she nor her mother had enjoyed the festival much for the last two years, though both had tried hard to disguise the fact. The best part was the dinner party which Dr Roberts gave for his friends and colleagues on Christmas Eve. He always had to carve the turkey at the hospital on the following day, and liked to have his own celebration behind him before that. Emma always chose to be on duty too, and Ruth came along to help with non-nursing jobs.

This year the weather was as un-Christmassy as it was possible to be. The springlike day on which Emma had met Craig had been followed by frost, which would have been fine a little later, but by Christmas Eve it had turned to heavy rain driven by a northerly gale.

Emma tried to cycle to the hospital as usual, but ended by walking most of the way. She arrived with her hair trickling down her neck and the lower part of her uniform dress clinging wetly to her legs. Luckily she always kept a spare at the hospital and so was able to change. When she came out of the cloakroom, tidy but still damp, she found Craig standing next to the big Christmas tree on the landing, taking off an anorak. His dark hair was wind-tossed but comparatively dry.

'You surely haven't been cycling!' he exclaimed.

Emma's heart had reacted uncomfortably to his unexpected appearance, but she managed to reply in a normal voice. 'I've been trying to! Did Rex get his walk this morning?'

'Not on the beach. It's impassable, owing to a very high tide caused by the gale. You can hear it pounding the cliffs all over the town, and it'll be even worse by the next high tide this evening.'

Emma had been concentrating so hard on her own battle with the elements that she hadn't realised how bad it must be on the coast and she immediately thought of Great-Aunt Mary.

'It'll be terribly noisy at Cliff House.' Glad of a safe topic for conversation, she pressed on with it. 'We've given up trying to persuade my old aunt to come to us for Christmas, but my mother is going to see her this afternoon to take her a few goodies, though goodness knows whether she'll eat them.'

'She really is an obstinate old so-and-so!' Craig exclaimed.

Emma had often thought of her aged relative like that but something made her rush to her defence. 'You have to admire her spirit, though.' Tilting her chin, she unwisely looked up into his face.

His eyes were fixed on hers and, for no reason at all, she felt herself colouring. Hastily, she changed the subject.

'What brings you here so early in the morning?'

'I admitted a motor-cyclist last night, after you'd gone off duty. He'd skidded taking a sharp bend too fast just outside the town. I couldn't discover anything wrong except bruises and concussion but I want to check up on him this morning.'

Maggie directed Emma to a bed near the door in a half-empty ward, where the Christmas decorations represented a snow scene very different from the muddy wetness outside. The boy was still asleep and, after studying his chart, Craig decided there was nothing to worry about.

'I'm going to keep him in over Christmas, though,' he told Emma. 'The concussion is severe and I don't feel I can trust an eighteen-year-old to stay in bed at home if he thinks he's well enough to get up.'

As they walked together out of the ward, he asked casually, 'Will you be at the party tonight?'

Emma's tone was equally casual. 'Oh, yes, and my mother too. Will you?'

'If I'm lucky, but I shall be on call.'

She made no comment, but she was conscious of a tiny, fragile hope that the inhabitants of Saxham might let Craig enjoy an undisturbed Christmas dinner.

When, hours later, she and Ruth arrived at Dr Roberts' house, it seemed at first that Emma might not get her wish. There was no sign of Craig. It was not until the twenty or so guests had moved from the drawing-room to seat themselves round the long dining-table that Emma's quick ears caught the sound of the front doorbell.

Impeccably dressed in a dark suit, looking well-groomed and leisured, and not in the least as though he had been visiting the sick, he slipped into a vacant seat a long way from Emma. She was unable to hear his murmured explanation to his hostess.

Dr Roberts hadn't heard it either, and he called down the table, 'Nothing serious, I hope, Craig?'

'Just a mystery rash on the youngest Coleman child. She seemed perfectly well and I decided it was something she'd eaten. I told her mother to keep an eye on her diet tomorrow, and hoped for the best.'

'It could even be due to over-excitement.' The elderly doctor took a sip of wine. 'Any improvement in the weather?'

'It's not raining so hard, but the wind is still blowing great guns.'

As Craig answered the question his eyes moved down the table and came to rest on Emma's face. She went on spooning up melon balls but she could just as easily have been eating pasta with no sauce for all the pleasure the taste gave her. Against her will, she met his gaze over a centre-piece of holly and Christmas roses, and she immediately sensed he had something he wanted to say to her.

Around them the conversation bubbled happily. They were as separated by laughter and talk as if there had been a glass screen between them. There was no chance of Craig being able to convey anything specific short of standing up and shouting.

It must be her imagination. What could he possibly want to tell her that was important enough to be said at a dinner party? There was only one thing she wanted to hear from him—I love you—and she was quite sure she would wait in vain for that.

The starter was cleared away, and the company sat back to admire the enormous turkey which was carried in by a buxom woman hired for the evening. It was followed by all the usual accompaniments, and later—much later—a plum pudding, blazing fitfully, mince pies and fruit.

Craig ate hungrily, though he drank very little, and talked animatedly with his neighbour on his

left, who was Dr Roberts' niece, come for
Christmas. She was an attractive blonde, and
Emma had met her before and liked her, but now
she hated her for holding Craig's attention.

At last, after what seemed an eternity, they left
the table and trooped back to the drawing-room
for coffee. Almost immediately Craig appeared
at Emma's side where she stood a little in the
background.

He wasted no time on preliminaries.

'Did your mother go to Cliff House today?'

She was surprised that he should have
remembered an odd bit of information like that.
'She went this afternoon. Why do you ask?'

'That child with the rash lives in one of the
bungalows on the other side of the track. I
stopped at your aunt's afterwards and walked
round to see the state of her garden. You'll be
glad to know it's still there.' He paused, but
Emma made no comment. 'I had a powerful torch
with me and I noticed that a piece of the cliff-edge
had vanished a little further along. I thought you
ought to know.'

'It was kind of you to take the trouble——'
Emma began.

He brushed her thanks impatiently aside. 'I do
feel most strongly that the old lady shouldn't be
left to spend the night there.'

'Are you prepared to carry her out kicking and
screaming?'

'I don't believe it would come to that,' Craig
said obstinately. 'All it needs is a tactful
approach.'

Emma raised her eyebrows. 'You just try being

tactful with Great-Aunt Mary and see where it gets you!'

'OK. I'm prepared to make the attempt, but you'll have to come with me.' He held her gaze, but all she could see was the lights of the Christmas tree reflected in his eyes.

'Of course I'll come, but it will be difficult to escape without causing a disturbance. . .' Her voice died away as she stood thinking.

Craig had instantly taken charge. 'I'll have a word with Dr Roberts and slip out first. There'll be no need for you to say anything to him.'

'I'd better tell my mother where we're going.'

It was all much easier than Emma had expected. People had not yet settled down after the meal, and most of the guests were standing about, holding coffee-cups. No one seemed to notice her own unobtrusive exit.

As she picked up her coat she remembered she would need keys, but luckily they were in her handbag. Putting them in her pocket, she looked down at the full-skirted, cream wool dress she was wearing and thought how unsuitable it was for going out on such a night on the sort of expedition this might turn out to be. With a shrug, she went out to join Craig. Great-Aunt Mary's safety was a great deal more important than a mere dress.

It was very dark outside and the wind was raging like a thousand demons, intermittently battering the car with large, fierce raindrops. Craig drove swiftly down a deserted High Street and turned up on to the cliff. Anxiously, Emma peered ahead, and saw, to her relief, the dim outline of the square, solid house, looking just as usual.

It was not until a few minutes later that they discovered everything *wasn't* just as usual.

When they got out of the car the wind snatched at them, and sent Emma's skirt whirling over her head so that she couldn't see and almost lost her footing.

Craig seized her arm and held it firmly. Together they staggered up the path towards the front door. In spite of the cold darkness, the threatening wind and waves, and the difficulty of their mission, Emma felt an odd sort of happiness and she wished the path were longer.

When they reached the porch Craig released her. 'I'll take a look round the back and join you again in a few minutes. You'll be OK if you stay here.'

'No!' Emma was suddenly consumed with anxiety. 'I'll come with you.'

'It's not in the least necessary.'

'Please——'

'Oh, all right.' He seized her arm again and they set off, walking as quickly as possible while they had the house beside them.

When they left its shelter the full force of the wind met them, and they were obliged to halt. It was as well that they did. A few yards ahead the torch showed them a horrific sight— a huge, yawning space filled with noise. The thundering waves below sounded as though they were climbing the cliff to reach them, and the scream of the wind was like a creature being tortured.

There were now only two or three feet left of Great Aunt Mary's garden.

Emma thought she heard herself scream, but it could have been the wind. Frantically, she clung to Craig as he stepped back, drawing her with him. Neither spoke until they were safe in the front porch.

'That settles it.' His voice was grim. 'There's no way we can leave the old lady here now.'

Emma unlocked the door with trembling fingers. The shock of what she had just seen was considerable, and even worse was the dread of what might be going to happen. Another landslide would definitely take at least part of the house with it.

Anxious not to alarm her great-aunt, she called out loudly as soon as they stepped into the hall. 'It's me, Aunt Mary—and Dr Norbury—we've come to see if you are all right.'

Silence. The house was like an island of stillness surrounded by roaring waters. They exchanged glances, and Emma read in his face the same fear she felt herself.

'She usually sits in the kitchen.' She moved towards it and opened the door. The electric fire glowed cheerfully and the armchair was in its usual place. So, too, was the old lady. 'Aunt Mary! Are you asleep?'

Craig passed her and reached the chair first. 'I don't think she's asleep,' he said in a low voice, his fingers on the shrunken wrist.

Emma joined him and he put his arm round her. She was trembling at this second shock and temporarily speechless.

'Didn't you tell me once she wanted to die in her own house?' he asked gently.

'It's what she always said when we tried to get her to move.' Emma struggled with a lump in her throat and his arm tightened. 'Do you think it was anything to do with the storm?' she asked when she could speak.

'No, I don't. I think her time had come.' He paused, and then added in a different tone, 'What a good thing she's been spared the trauma of being taken away from her home on such a night—against her will too, very probably. At her age this is the best thing that could have happened.'

Emma fumbled for a handkerchief and rubbed her eyes. Great-Aunt Mary had been here for so long—all Emma's own life and ages before that—and now her spirit had fled and left behind only this dreadfully still shell of a living, breathing, determined old lady.

'What you need,' came Craig's voice just above her head, 'is a drop of brandy, but I don't suppose there's any here?'

'There is, actually. My aunt always kept a small bottle in the bathroom cupboard—for medicinal purposes, she insisted.' Reluctantly, Emma disentangled herself from his comforting arm. 'I'll fetch it.'

The bathroom was a comparatively modern addition, built on at the back. Miss Mayfield hadn't really wanted it, but for once had given in to family pressure. The noise of the storm was worse in there, due to the walls being thinner, and Emma hunted feverishly for the brandy in the cupboard above the washbasin. Aspirin, cough mixture, rheumatism cream—there it was, right at the back.

Her middle was pressed against the basin and suddenly she felt it move. Trying to pretend she'd imagined it, she glanced nervously round. At the same moment the noise increased to a deep, thundering roar, and the floor under her feet shifted. Before her terrified eyes, the wall nearest the sea fell away, leaving a dark space into which the bath promptly disappeared.

The landslide stopped, leaving the lino flapping in the gap. Clinging to the basin, Emma was paralysed with terror, afraid to try and reach the hall in case she speeded up the destruction of the bathroom. Another fall would take her over the edge with it, down to the hungry waves below. And that could only mean the end of everything.

Why didn't Craig come? Surely he must have heard the noise?

He was there in the hall. She could see him through the open door. He called out, 'Emma—oh, my God——' and advanced as far as the threshold.

She screamed at him, 'Be careful—oh, do be careful!'

His face was ashen, but he had recaptured his composure. 'You can't stay there, love.' His voice was tense but quite calm. 'Move very slowly towards me and I'll stretch out a hand to help you. I daren't come any farther, in case my weight is too much for the floor—gently, now.'

Emma loosened her panic grip on the washbasin and did exactly as she had been told. Her legs were shaking so much that she had to steady herself with a hand on the wall until she could reach Craig's outstretched arm. Slowly, slowly she inched along, and then—at last—she was safe in his grasp.

'Let's get as far from the back as possible.' He drew her along the hall, still holding her tightly, and came to a halt near the front door. 'Oh, Emma darling——' his arms enfolded her '—I can still hardly believe you're safe! When I heard that terrible noise, and realised what it was, I thought you'd gone over the cliff too. I hardly dared to come and look—and when I saw you still there, unhurt, I wanted to rush in and carry you away, back to safety.'

Emma listened in a daze. Was Craig really saying all those wonderful things? Or was she hallucinating due to shock? And when he smoothed her hair back and kissed her eyes, the tip of her nose, and finally her lips, she stood like a statue in his arms, unable to believe.

He released her abruptly. 'I'm sorry—I'm afraid I got a bit carried away. But the relief was so tremendous I couldn't help it.' His eyes held her gaze and there was an infinite sadness in their depths. 'I love you so very much, Emma dear, and until Paul came back I thought there was hope you might be getting over what he did to you and would soon be ready to trust another man.'

Emma burst out, 'I had got over it, Craig—I really had——'

'But when you saw him again, and he was so ill and needed all your nursing skills, your love came back, didn't it?' Before she could answer he went rushing on. 'And then it all happened again—you found out he was married, and once more you had to pick up the pieces and try to mend your life.'

This time Emma managed to make herself heard. 'Please, please will you stop romanticising and listen to me? You've got it all wrong! I didn't fall in love with Paul all over again—I was very sorry for him because he could have died, but that's not the same as loving him.' She took a deep breath and summoned all her courage. 'There's only one man I love, and he's so determined to cast me in the role of heartbroken, abandoned heroine that he won't listen to what I'm trying to tell him.' With an effort she produced a quivering smile.

'You what?' Craig stared down at her, his eyes raking her face. 'I don't understand.'

Emma stood on tiptoe, getting as close to him as she could. She put up her arms and linked her hands behind his head. 'It's *you* I love, not Paul, and you've been making me very unhappy these last few weeks because I thought you'd only been playing around.' Her eyes were bright with unshed tears. 'I'm still afraid to believe I got it all wrong too.'

There was a brief, stunned silence and then Craig smiled. 'Would you say we've been behaving like a couple of idiots?' And when she laughed and agreed, he swung her off her feet, his mouth eager to capture the sweetness of her lips in the full knowledge of their mutual love.

It was the noise of the storm which brought them back to their senses. It was so clearly neither the time nor the place for love, and there was the body of Great-Aunt Mary to be dealt with. It was obviously impossible to leave her where she was.

'If you wouldn't mind helping me,' Craig said, 'we could move her, in her chair, as far from the back of the house as possible.'

'That would be the parlour—it hasn't been used for years.'

'OK—it will do fine. She ought to be safe there for the present. A large slice of cliff has already gone and I don't think there'll be another fall just yet. My mobile phone is in the car and I'll summon an ambulance to take her to the mortuary at the hospital.'

'Poor Aunt Mary, she's been an institution for so long that I can't believe she's no longer here.'

'She died as she would have wanted,' Craig reminded her gently. He took her hand and drew her towards the kitchen. 'Come on, love, let's get it over.'

The old lady looked so exactly as she had done in life that Emma scarcely found her removal macabre at all. Within a few minutes, she and Craig were driving away through the storm.

'Do you want to go back to the party?' he asked quietly.

Until then Emma hadn't even thought that far ahead. Now she knew quite definitely that it was the last thing she wanted. 'No, I don't! It—it seems all wrong somehow.'

'I take it you don't want to drive around in the rain?' There was a smile in his voice.

'It doesn't sound very attractive.' Emma hesitated. 'Would it be a good idea to go to our

house for a little while? It'll be nice and warm
and—dry.'

'I think it would be a very good idea.' His hand
touched hers briefly, sending her pulses racing,
and he peered at his watch by the light of a street-
lamp. 'We've got about an hour. A lot can happen
in sixty minutes.'

The tiny house in Little Back Lane was cosy
and welcoming, and the flickering firelight in the
sitting-room needed no further illumination.

As Craig sat down on the sofa and drew her
close, Emma felt dizzy with happiness. As he
kissed and caressed her passionately, and she
responded, she wished they could stay there
together for a long, long time and not have to
return to the real world, with its obligations and
worries and—other people.

'Do you know what I want?' Craig murmured.

It wasn't hard to guess, because Emma wanted
it too, and she made no reply.

'I want to make love to you, Emma, darling,
and I can't because I'm on call. So you'd better
stop being so tempting or I might not be able to
resist.'

'Perhaps we ought to have a conversation about
something?' she suggested, laughing.

'Good idea. There's plenty to talk about, but
first things first. I've been thinking what a good
thing it is that you love my dog as well as me,
because I couldn't possibly marry anyone who
didn't.'

Emma raised her head from his shoulder and
looked into his face. 'You do want to marry
me, then?'

'Of course I do! Didn't I tell you?'

'Not that I recall.'

'Well, I'm saying it now. Would you like me to go down on my knee and propose properly?'

'Idiot!' She laughed softly, and it was a few minutes before the conversation was resumed.

'I also want you to have a proper engagement-ring,' he went on eventually, 'and you will be married in white, won't you, darling? I'd like us to have a real old-fashioned wedding at the local church.'

When Emma had finished assuring him that she wanted exactly the same, she suddenly remembered the beautiful white dress she had bought for the ball and never worn. With slight alterations it would make a lovely wedding-gown. After all, people often turned a wedding-dress into one for evening, so why not the other way round?

'A spring wedding would be lovely,' she said dreamily. 'Don't you think so?'

'I don't care when it is, so long as it's soon.'

'There's a lot to be settled,' Emma pointed out. 'Where are we going to live? Do you want me to move into the flat?'

Craig thought about it, frowning a little. 'It might be OK for a short time, while we look round and choose something else at our leisure.' He paused. 'There's another thing to be discussed. Are you going to continue nursing?'

Emma hadn't got as far as that in her thinking. Everything had happened so quickly, she hadn't caught up.

'I certainly don't want to give up,' she

said slowly. 'Perhaps I could become a part-timer?'

'With no night duty,' Craig put in firmly, and kissed her long and hard. 'I want my wife in bed beside me every night, and if I'm unlucky enough to be called out I'd like to know she'll be there, keeping it warm for me.'

'You're expecting to get welcomed back with frozen hands and feet?'

The thought was so intoxicating to them both that all practical discussion abruptly ceased. Eventually, Emma disentangled herself.

'It's nearly time for us to go, love. Dr Roberts was going to drive Mum and me home at the end of the party, and I must appear before then.'

'I suppose so.' Craig sat up reluctantly. 'I'll be able to save him a journey anyway.'

'He'll be grateful,' Emma said absently. Something had just come into her head—the petition. She had actually forgotten it for a whole evening.

'What's the matter?' he asked, instantly sensing her slight withdrawal.

'Nothing, really. It's just that I suddenly thought of the petition.' She hesitated. 'Will you be very angry if I make a suggestion about it?'

'I shall probably beat you black and blue, but don't let that stop you. What is it?'

'I wondered if I could take it to the office of the Health Services Trust when we go to Heathbury to choose my ring? I do realise it's a lot to ask, when you don't agree with it at all, but it would take me all day to get there and back without a car.' She went close and put a hand on his arm. 'Would you mind very much?'

Craig was so long answering that she got nervous.

'I've got something to tell you,' he said at last, 'but I certainly didn't intend to raise the subject this evening. I heard yesterday on the grapevine that there's to be a definite announcement made directly after the New Year. They've chosen the site for the new hospital, Emma dear, and architects' plans are being drawn up for a building large enough to replace both Stonebridge and Saxham. Work will probably start quite soon.' He took her hand and held it tightly. 'I'm very sorry to give you such a disappointment after all your hard work.'

'Others worked too,' she reminded him bleakly.

'But you did most of it. Unfortunately—from your point of view—it was too late.'

Emma gave a long sigh and said goodbye to her dreams of influencing the decisions of the authorities. 'What shall I do with the petition, then?' she asked sadly. 'It represents hours and hours of work, and the opinions of more people than perhaps you realise. It shouldn't be wasted.'

'It certainly shouldn't, and I think you should take it to Heathbury as you suggested just now. It could make the people in charge realise that there's a lot to be said for keeping on the old people's day centre. They might even decide to build a clinic for Saxham, and that would be a considerable achievement.'

'It certainly would!' Emma stood up and tried to smooth her hair. 'We really must go, love.' She smiled. 'At least on a night like this no one will be surprised to see us looking dishevelled.'

Craig grinned and tucked her into her coat. 'Who cares what they think? We've got a bigger surprise than that in store for them!'

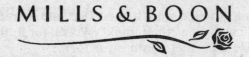

MILLS & BOON

LOVE ON CALL

The books for enjoyment this month are:

MIDWIFE'S DILEMMA	Lilian Darcy
MADE FOR EACH OTHER	Elizabeth Harrison
HOSPITAL AT RISK	Clare Lavenham
SEEING EYE TO EYE	Josie Metcalfe

Treats in store!

Watch next month for the following absorbing stories:

NEVER SAY NEVER	Margaret Barker
DANGEROUS PHYSICIAN	Marion Lennox
THE CALL OF DUTY	Jessica Matthews
FLIGHT INTO LOVE	Meredith Webber

Available from W.H. Smith, John Menzies, Volume One, Forbuoys,
Martins, Tesco, Asda, Safeway and other paperback stockists.

Readers in South Africa - write to:
IBS, Private Bag X3010, Randburg 2125.

A years supply of Mills & Boon romances — absolutely free!

Would you like to win a years supply of heartwarming and passionate romances? Well, you can and they're FREE! All you have to do is complete the word puzzle below and send it to us by 29th February 1996. The first 5 correct entries picked out of the bag after that date will win a years supply of Mills & Boon romances (six books every month—worth over £100). What could be easier?

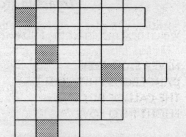

GMWIMSIN

NNSAUT

ACEHB

EMSMUR

ANCOE

DNSA

RTOISTU

THEOL

ATYCH

NSU

MYSTERY DESTINATION

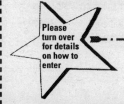

Please turn over for details on how to enter